"Go on, what's it say?" Hildy nudged her.

Belinda unfolded the paper, smiling at her own foolishness.

And then the smile froze on her lips.

"What is it?" Hildy was watching her, and suddenly none of it was funny anymore.

"It's . . . it's a page from a calendar. April." Belinda let the paper flutter from her fingers. "Oh, God—"

Frank snatched up the page as Belinda sagged back in her chair.

"What is that, Frank?" she asked tonelessly. And he stared at her, not answering, his face suddenly unsure. "That mark, Frank — that mark on the first of April — Frank, *what is that?*"

And his mouth moved, but nothing came out, and Belinda shut her eyes and said it again.

"That circle around April Fools' Day, Frank — April Fools' Day—"

"It couldn't be," Frank said quietly. "It looks like . . . like dried blood."

**Other Point Horror
Paperbacks you will enjoy:**

Point Horror

APRIL FOOLS

Richie Tankersley Cusick

Hippo Books
Scholastic Children's Books
London

To Dorothy . . .

for those before
and those to come
and especially for your friendship

Scholastic Children's Books,
Scholastic Publications Ltd,
7-9 Pratt Street, London NW1 0AE, UK

Scholastic Inc.,
730 Broadway, New York, NY 10003, USA

Scholastic Canada Ltd,
123 Newkirk Road, Richmond Hill,
Ontario Canada, L4C 3G5

Ashton Scholastic Pty Ltd,
P O Box 579, Gosford, New South Wales,
Australia

Ashton Scholastic Ltd,
Private Bag 1, Penrose, Auckland,
New Zealand

First published in the US by Scholastic Inc., 1990
First published in the UK by Scholastic Publications Ltd, 1991

Copyright © Richie Tankersley Cusick, 1990

ISBN 0 590 76420 9

10 9 8 7

Prologue

Later, when Belinda thought about that horrible night, she could think of a hundred "if only's" that might have made things turn out differently. *If only we hadn't gone to that party.* . . . She hated parties anyway, and Hildy had been grounded — why in the world had she ever told Hildy she'd go along in the first place? She hadn't even known the people who'd been giving the stupid party — some college buddies of Frank's older brother — and once she and Hildy and Frank had gotten there, she'd known right away there was too much drinking going on. *If only we hadn't gone . . . if only it hadn't been out of town.* . . . She'd told her mother that she was spending the night at Hildy's just like any other weekend, that they'd just stay in and rent some movies. *If only we hadn't tried to drive there and back again. If only Frank hadn't drunk all those beers.* . . .

If only it hadn't been April Fools' Day.

Because, really, that's what had started the whole thing off — that stupid April Fools' Day party. That, and Frank being an even bigger jerk than usual, appointing himself the official King of Fools, much to everyone's delight. Frank had never needed an excuse to make a total fool of himself, but this time he'd been so outrageous that Belinda had been embarrassed for him. She'd actually been relieved when he'd gotten so drunk that Hildy insisted they leave. And she remembered how Hildy had fought him when Frank wouldn't give up the car keys, and how much trouble they'd had pouring him into the front seat, how terrified they'd been when he'd grabbed the wheel, weaving them all over the road.

If only . . . if only everything had been different.

But things hadn't been different, and afterward she could still see everything so clearly . . . *too* clearly.

She and Frank and Hildy driving home so late that night . . . and the terrible storm beating down on them . . . They'd taken a shortcut — some little used road near the airport — that Frank's brother had suggested, where there wasn't likely to be any highway patrol on the lookout for late party-goers and . . . Hildy had gotten more and more upset because Frank kept trying to drive. . . . Frank had started feeling sick, but there was nowhere to pull off on the narrow downhill stretch, and it was so curvy and dangerous, and Belinda had been so frightened. . . . That's when the other car had pulled up behind them, honking, trying to pass. Belinda had peered out through the streaming rain on the back window, but hadn't been able to see any faces, and the car had kept honking and honking and Frank had gotten mad.

"Let's give those hotshots a scare," he'd said, and Belinda had felt like she was choking, thick bands of fear tightening around her chest, that awful premonition that something horrible was about to happen. She'd begged Hildy to pull over and let the car pass, and Hildy had really tried, but Frank had suddenly grabbed the wheel again, and they'd almost run the other car off the road. She remembered Hildy shouting at him, and Frank saying, "Let's give them a *real* scare this time!" and how he'd leaned on the horn and started laughing.

She could still see it. Even now.

The other car swerving around them, just as Frank's foot hit the gas pedal, lurching them forward, right onto the other car's fender. Faster and faster — and Hildy had started hitting him, wrestling Frank for the steering wheel, and Belinda had closed her eyes and prayed, certain they were all going to die. Just Hildy yelling and Frank laughing and the squeal of tires on slick blacktop as they'd slid around curves, hot on the tail of the car in front — and Belinda begging them to stop — *begging* — begging them to let her out of the car —

"Frank, *don't!*" She'd joined the fight then, prying his fingers from the wheel. "Someone's going to get *hurt!* It's not *funny!*"

"Oh, lighten up, Belinda! It's April Fools' Day, and I can do what I want. Hey — nothing can happen to me — I'm King of Fools! What the hell — they can't just push the king around like I'm a nobody! I'm teaching them a little lesson in respect. Tell you what, I won't even write them a speeding ticket, whatcha say?"

And then it happened.

Right then, right in front of their eyes.

The other car disappeared.

One minute it was in front of them, taillights swishing through the curtain of rain . . .

The next minute the road was black and empty.

"What — stop the car, Hildy — *stop the car!*" And Belinda was never sure if she'd really said the words out loud or just in her head because the noise had come then — the terrible, unbelievable noise not so far away — the crash going on and on through the dark and the thunder, and the crunching and twisting of metal, and the helpless, panicky screams —

My God, those awful screams —

For a moment time had ended. She remembered Hildy frozen in the front seat . . . Frank's dazed, white face. . . . She could feel the rain pounding on the roof, like her heart pounding in her throat —

"Oh, God! Hurry!"

"No, Belinda, wait —"

"Come on!"

And somehow she'd found it — or what was left of it — the mangled car at the bottom of the gorge, the sudden flicker of light, a small burst of flames —

"We've got to help!" She'd been half out of her mind, running toward the wreck like that, slipping and falling over the rocks, sliding down the muddy hill. "We've got to help —"

4

It had taken her a while to even realize that Frank and Hildy weren't behind her. She remembered whirling around and hearing her name being called over and over from the darkness . . . seeing them struggling over the rocks, trying to catch up . . .

While someone watched from the top of the hill.

Even now it made her skin crawl.

Because someone had been up there in front of their car, caught in the weak blur of the headlights, a person — a man — just standing beside the car, just standing there, watching them —

"Help!" Belinda had screamed, and she'd started back again, waving her arms — "Help us! *Please!*"

But he hadn't moved, and so she'd run on, run straight on to the burning car, and had almost reached it when Frank finally tackled her, throwing her to the ground, and she'd kept screaming, and someone *else* had been screaming, too.

Not Hildy, whose face was soaked with rain and tears, not Frank who kept yelling, "It's gonna *blow* — let's get *out* of here — the whole thing's gonna go *up!*"

But other screams — screams of pain and terror — and in the growing rush of crackling light, she'd seen the outline of someone — someone still alive — moving against the flames, trapped upside down behind the car window —

And *"NO!"* Belinda shrieked. She'd tried to claw Hildy and Frank away, as they'd pulled on her, forcing her up the hill —

They'd heard the explosion, felt the earth tremble beneath them, and she'd tried to turn around and go back, but Frank had shoved her so hard, she'd fallen to the ground in front of the head-lights. . . .

The mushy ground where two footprints were filling up with water . . .

"Someone was here," she'd mumbled, "Hildy, someone was here — do you see him? Where'd he go?"

"Come *on*, Belinda, there's nobody — we've got to get *out* of here —"

"But Hildy, someone —"

"Come on, get in the car!"

She hadn't really thought as she'd reached out for the muddy rag beside her on the ground . . . she'd gone into a sort of numbness, hands reaching out and pushing her, and the warm taste of blood in her mouth and on her lips as she'd pressed the cold, wet rag against her aching face.

She remembered the rain . . . beating down on them without mercy.

And Frank babbling over and over like an idiot, "It was just a joke . . . a *joke*."

My God, what have we done. . . .

If only it hadn't been April Fools' Day.

If only the screams would stop echoing forever and ever in her mind.

Chapter 1

"Frank and I are worried about you," Hildy said, popping a french fry into her mouth. "You're acting kind of depressed."

"Well, that's silly, isn't it? What could I *possibly* have to be depressed about?" Belinda gave her friend a wry smile, then sighed as Hildy leaned forward and slapped her palm down on the table.

"Snap out of it, will you? It's over with. It's been two weeks, and it's over with. Besides, we made a pact and you can't break it."

"He shouldn't have done it," Belinda mumbled.

"For God's sake, it was a stupid joke! You know Frank — it was April Fools' Day, and he was the King of Fools! He doesn't take anything seriously on *normal* days." She studied the other girl with an exasperated sigh. "You're really being dramatic about this. Your mom's gonna start asking dumb questions if you don't watch it."

"Mom's working double shifts at the hospital again. We never even see each other. Look, Hildy," Belinda spread her hands, searching for the right words. "Someone was trapped in that car. I still see him, being burned alive. We were . . . responsible —"

"Oh, come on, we didn't make them miss the road. Those people should have been watching where they were going!"

"It's never even been on the news — I keep waiting and waiting —"

"It was a two-hour drive from here! There's no reason why an accident that happened a hundred miles away should even be *mentioned* on the local news! Car wrecks happen every day —"

"But they don't have anything to do with us!"

"And this doesn't, either. You're acting like this is some huge tragedy or something and —"

"It *is* a tragedy! I just keep — keep *feeling* that somehow we'll be . . . paid back for what we did."

"How many times do I have to tell you, we didn't do *anything*. And we stopped at that gas station, didn't we? Well, *didn't* we? It wasn't our fault it was closed and the stupid pay phone was broken. Jeez, you're driving me nuts!"

Belinda's voice dropped, her eyes unhappy. "I can't get away from it, Hildy. I dream about it. We should have tried harder to get help. We should have gone to the police —"

Hildy bent low, her mouth pressed into an angry line. "Oh, right, what a smart thing to do. You know Frank was drunk — he wasn't even supposed to *be* at that party! If Coach Jarvis found out Frank was there instead of at that special swim practice . . . I mean, Frank called in *sick* and *lied* to him! He could be thrown off the team! And *I* was grounded — I shouldn't have been there, either. *You*, either. If you remember, we were *supposed* to be house-sitting while my parents were out of town." The anger melted, replaced by a quiet pleading that Belinda could never resist. "Do you know how much trouble we'd have been in if we'd gone to the cops? I don't even want to think about what they'd have done to Frank in his condition — and if my parents found out about *any* of it, they'd *never* let me date Frank again. Look . . . we did all we could."

"But what about the man I saw up on the hill?" Belinda said stubbornly. "Someone *saw* us there —"

"There wasn't anyone there, I've told you a hundred times. Look, it was raining, you were upset —"

"Hildy, someone was there. I didn't imagine it."

"Okay. Suppose this guy *was* there. He'll just think we stopped to help — which we *did*, by the way. And why didn't *he* hang around anyway? Why didn't *he* try to help?"

"Maybe he did. Maybe he went and called an ambulance."

"Then what are you *worried* about?"

Belinda shook her head slowly. "Maybe he saw us chasing the car. Maybe he thinks we pushed it off the cliff. Maybe he got the license number —"

"Oh, Belinda —" Hildy looked impatient but tried to keep her voice reasonable. "We've been all over this before. Nobody's come around asking anything, have they?" Belinda shook her head reluctantly. "Okay. I just don't think there *was* a man. Frank and I didn't see *anyone*."

"I saw footprints."

"All three of us walked around in front of the car — there were probably *lots* of footprints —" Hildy bit her lip, and Belinda could almost hear her mentally counting to ten. "I know you've been under a strain — studying, and doing everything at home — and you must be tutoring half the school for exams —"

"Not half," Belinda almost smiled at that. "Almost, but not half —"

"Your advertising sure works. All the cards you posted at school and around town — I don't know how you stand it."

"We need the money, Hildy. I don't have a choice."

"Yeah . . . well . . ." Hildy looked uncomfortable and hurried on. "Mrs. Larson at the library said some guy even asked about you the other day. He saw your card there and wanted to know something about you, so she showed him your picture in the yearbook and told him how qualified you are —"

A twinge of fear hit her, though she wasn't quite sure why. "Who was he?"

"She didn't know. But I guess that means he'll be calling you."

Belinda nodded uncertainly.

"So . . . what? Aren't you glad? This might be Mister Right, you know, just walking into your life and . . . what's the matter?"

Belinda shook her head. No matter what, her mind kept going back to the accident, and she didn't want to start Hildy off again.

"I've gotta get to class." Hildy shoved back her chair, long silvery braids brushing across the tabletop, pale green eyes narrowed on Belinda like a cat's. "You'd better get your act together. You're getting to be a real bore with all this."

Belinda gave a vague nod and watched her go, Hildy's miniskirted figure sashaying through the crowded cafeteria and drawing the usual stares. "If it was some problem with cheerleading, you'd be panic-stricken," Belinda grumbled, then stopped herself, ashamed. She and Hildy were best friends, after all. Hildy had never been one to dwell over problems; Hildy hated little annoyances upsetting her busy social life. Belinda had always been the worrier. While Hildy was going out on all the dates, Belinda sat home, worrying about studying, about making money for college, about how she was going to help Hildy pass her next big test. But that was okay, wasn't it? Best friends accepted each other unconditionally, didn't they?

Sighing, Belinda gathered up her books and tossed her empty juice can into the trash by the door. Every time she tried to eat lately, she felt queasy. Better to go on to gym and grab something afterward that she could munch between classes. She checked her watch and began hurrying across campus when suddenly the intercom crackled to life, bellowing its message through the entire school.

"Belinda Swanson — please report to the office immediately — Belinda Swanson — to the office —"

It was as if someone had punched her. Freezing in midstride, Belinda grabbed her stomach and fought off a wave of nausea. *They know! They know we killed that person in that car!* Her mind raced in a million directions, but as she took a deep breath, a frail thread of calm fought for control. *How could they know? Just go to the office and see what they want. Act normal. They couldn't possibly know . . .*

She felt like a wooden doll going back across the yard and into the administration building. She wondered if Hildy and Frank had heard the intercom and what they were thinking. Stopping at the main desk, she leaned forward, her mouth so cottony that she couldn't even talk. The secretary gave her a smile and motioned her toward the principal's door.

"Go on in, Belinda — Mr. Grumes is expecting you."

And she couldn't quite recall getting into his office, but then Mr. Grumes was nodding at her from his oversized desk and waving her into a chair while he hastily finished a conversation on the phone.

Someone else was in the room, too — a tall, severe-looking woman in the chair beside Belinda's. She was dressed in black — suit, shoes, even her hat — the veil of the hat had been lifted slightly, to reveal cold eyes. She looked about fortyish, Belinda thought, but there were bruises on her cheeks, which showed through layers and layers of makeup.

Her ringed fingers tapped nervously on the arms of her chair, and as the color began to drain from Belinda's face, the woman gave her a long, hard stare.

"Belinda —" Mr. Grumes leaned over and shook her hand — "nice to see you. I wasn't sure if you'd dressed for gym yet or not — glad I caught you in time."

Belinda forced a smile, hoping it didn't look fake. "I was just on my way."

"Well, I won't keep you in suspense, though I'm sure *you'd* never be afraid you're in any kind of trouble." Mr. Grumes gave her a knowing look, and Belinda squirmed against the sticky leather seat. "Belinda, this is Mrs. Thorne . . . and Mrs. Thorne, this is the young lady you were asking about."

Belinda nodded and felt the woman's eyes boring into her, as if searching for her very soul.

"Mrs. Thorne is interested in hiring a tutor," Mr. Grumes went on in his businesslike way. "So when she called the school about you, I suggested she meet you for herself."

He paused, and Belinda felt herself sinking back against the cushions, a long, slow breath draining all the fear from her heart. She closed her eyes and opened them again, meeting the woman's stare.

"It's my stepson. My husband's child." Mrs. Thorne's voice was low and agitated. "He's been . . . ill . . . and it's . . . impossible for him to attend school at the present time. His mother doesn't want him falling behind in his studies, so I'm trying to find a . . . a tutor for the boy —"

"Belinda's our best student," Mr. Grumes broke in. "Mature . . . dependable . . . she's very good with people —"

"My husband's business takes up most of my time," Mrs. Thorne cut him off. "I work long hours and have to do a great deal of traveling, especially now. It was the boy's mother who wanted to send him here — it wasn't my idea." She paused, looking irritated with the whole situation. "My husband's in the hospital at present; he mustn't be disturbed or upset. I thought if you could come in several times a week . . . work with the boy on school assignments . . . his mother wants him kept in touch with the outside world —" She stopped herself abruptly. Belinda had the distinct feeling she was holding something back. "Of course I understand you must be very busy . . . I'd be willing to pay you generously for your time."

Belinda thought quickly — all the scrimping and saving she'd had to do ever since Mom and Dad's divorce . . . the painstaking struggle just to make ends meet. She really needed money for college in the fall. And Mom worked so hard all the time . . . *and it's not like I don't have any experience — all those baby-sitting jobs, the hours of volunteer work at the hospital — with a little juggling I could fit this one in.*

"And if you'd like to meet my stepson before deciding," Mrs. Thorne looked away, "that can easily be arranged."

Mr. Grumes nodded emphatically. "His own school's compiled some lesson plans for him — I've looked them over myself, and you shouldn't have any trouble —"

"Mr. Grumes tells me you've done tutoring for lots of other children —"

"Yes, just about every age group." Belinda gave a modest smile.

"She seems to have a magic touch," the principal said smoothly, "for always squeaking the really terrible students by." He gave her a sly wink and Belinda reddened, thinking of Hildy.

"I hear he's very bright," Mrs. Thorne went on, not looking particularly impressed, "although at this particular time . . . well . . . he's been rather depressed. He's also difficult. His mother's at a loss with what to do with him — she has a job herself and can't stay home — she thought a change of scene might be beneficial."

"You think about it," Mr. Grumes added, reaching for the buzzing telephone. "You think about it and let us know —"

"If I could just have your answer by the end of the week," Mrs. Thorne said crisply. "So I can make other arrangements for the boy if you decide you can't do it —"

"Of course she'll do it, won't you, Belinda? You'll be great!" Belinda opened her mouth to protest, but Mr. Grumes rushed on. "I have every confidence in you. If anyone can make a difference with the kid, you can." He grinned at her, then spoke into the receiver, their discussion obviously at an end.

"Maybe I *should* meet him first," Belinda stood up, speaking softly to Mrs. Thorne, who was gathering her purse and jacket. "If he's really having that bad of a time, maybe we should all be sure he wants me there —"

"He doesn't know *what* he wants — *or* what he needs," Mrs. Thorne replied tartly, then hesitated, thinking. "Cobbs is in town this afternoon, and I have that meeting — Oh, very well, I suppose I'll just have to be late. Give me your address."

Slightly dismayed, Belinda took the pen and paper offered her and wrote down the information, handing it back with an apologetic smile.

"I just wouldn't want him upset, you know, having me there. It always seems to bring out the worst in kids when they get stuck with a baby-sitter they can't stand."

The woman, walking a few steps ahead of her, turned in surprise. "Were you under the impression that he's a small child?"

This time it was Belinda's turn to look surprised. "Well, when you said it was your stepson . . . the way you were talking about him . . . I just thought —"

Her smile was tight. "You and my stepson are probably near the same age."

"Oh . . . well . . ."

"Adam Thorne," she said. "He just turned eighteen. In spite of the accident."

The woman's tone of voice chilled Belinda, and she stared at Mrs. Thorne, as if from a long way off.

"Adam . . . was in an accident?" she asked weakly.

"You're a very polite girl, but you must have noticed my injuries. It's a miracle I lived through it at all. It's a miracle any of us did." They came out into the daylight and Mrs. Thorne adjusted her black veil with trembling fingers. "My husband isn't going to make it, Belinda." Her voice sank to a bitter whisper. "And now I'm stuck with Adam. All because of that car accident two weeks ago."

Chapter 2

When Belinda got to her locker, Hildy was already there waiting for her.

"Belinda! God, what happened? I heard the intercom and —"

"We've got to talk," Belinda said. She grabbed her books and steered Hildy outside, weaving through the swarms of students heading for home. As they ducked beneath an outside stairwell, Belinda glanced around to make sure they hadn't been noticed, while Hildy huddled there looking frightened.

"Belinda, tell me. Is it about . . . you know . . ."

"Mr. Grumes wants me to tutor some boy. Hildy, the guy's a senior, and he can't go to school."

Hildy stared at her. "So? Is he contagious or something?"

"*No!* He was in a car wreck *two weeks ago*." Belinda stepped back, waiting for her friend's reaction — panic, guilt, *something* — but Hildy still looked blank. Belinda grabbed her shoulder and shook her. "Did you hear me? Did you hear what I said —"

"Hey, what's going on?" Frank suddenly appeared out of nowhere and slipped between them, his handsome features locked in a frown. "Is this a fight? No hair pulling or blouse ripping without the referee." He grinned wickedly and looked down at Belinda. "So what was that little trip to Grumes's office all about?"

For a moment neither girl spoke. Then Hildy began to laugh as Belinda gazed on in disbelief.

"Hildy, this is *not* funny! Don't you under —"

"Oh, but it *is* funny." Hildy couldn't stop giggling, and Frank leaned back, watching them both in growing amusement. "It's funny 'cause you're so predictable! Oh, poor Belinda — I'm sorry, but —"

"So what's this great joke, anyway?" Frank demanded. "What'd I miss?"

"It's not a joke," Belinda said quietly. She stared down at the ground, praying she wouldn't start to cry. She always cried at the wrong times. And then they'd just make fun of her some more, and *why can't they see how serious this is*. . . . She felt Hildy's hand on her arm and reluctantly raised her eyes.

"Belinda, look, it's just so funny, I —"

"It's not funny, Hildy. It's horrible. Don't you see what it means?"

"No, I don't. But I *thought*, by the way you were acting, that . . . well, you know. I'm just so *relieved*, you scared me half to death —"

"Well, great, but will one of you please tell *me* what's going on, so I can share in all this fun?" Frank crossed his arms over his chest, and Hildy gave Belinda an encouraging pat.

"Go on. Start at the beginning."

Belinda swallowed . . . nodded. "Some woman came to see Mr. Grumes. Her stepson's staying with her, and he needs a tutor." They were staring at her so intently now that she paused, and Frank shifted his gaze briefly to Hildy's.

"Well, okay, so what?"

"I'm not sure what's wrong with him, but he can't go to school. The woman — Mrs. Thorne — had bruises on her face and said her husband's dying — all from this car accident they were in two weeks ago." Belinda stopped, pressed her hand to her mouth. For a moment there was just the soft popping of Hildy's gum.

"Belinda —" Frank said carefully, "you don't *really* think —"

"Two weeks, Frank. *Two weeks!*"

"Yeah, okay, I know, but wrecks happen every single day and what're the chances of —"

"Where did it happen?" Hildy butted in. "Did she say where it happened?"

"Well . . . no."

"Then it could have been anywhere. Frank's right, Belinda, I think you're really stretching it."

"Give it a rest, huh?" Frank patted her on the back. "You're making yourself crazy for no reason. You're seeing ghosts in every corner."

Belinda looked back at them, reading their patronizing expressions. She sighed and turned away. "I'm not going to take the job."

"But why not?" Hildy hurried to catch up with her as she strode across the yard toward the street. "It sounds like an easy way to make money, doesn't it? It'd be a snap for you. What's the guy's name?"

Belinda sidestepped a puddle, heard Frank splash through it, heard Hildy's squeal as mud splattered her stockings. "Adam, I think. Adam Thorne."

"Adam . . ." Hildy sighed to herself. "Ooh, that sounds so romantic. Look, Belinda, if I were you —"

You'd have a conscience, she wanted to say, but instead she bit her tongue as Hildy kept chattering.

"I'd at least see what this Adam guy looks like. I mean, this could be *it*, this could be THE ONE, if you know what I mean, and then I wouldn't have to worry about you being so alone all the time —"

"You *don't* worry," Belinda said offhandedly. "Since when do you worry?"

"Hildy's right." Frank wagged a finger at her. "All work and no play makes Belinda a very dull —"

"And anyway, what would you tell Mr. Grumes?" Hildy persisted. "If you say you won't do it, he might wonder why and start asking questions and —"

"He'll put the pressure on you" — Frank popped his knuckles and grinned — "and you'll crack —"

"Oh, please." Belinda quickened her pace. She was not in the mood for Frank's perverse humor, but his strong hands clamped down on her shoulders, forcing her around.

"Hey, what's with you anyway?" He flashed that irresistible grin. "You used to *love* my jokes. You used to love *me*." He loosened his hold on her arms, tilting her face up so he could look into her eyes, and Belinda blushed and looked away. There had been a time she would have given anything for a date with Frank Scaleri, anything just to have him notice her. But it had been Hildy who Frank had noticed, Hildy who Frank had fallen head over heels for, just like all the other guys in school always had. Always Hildy. Belinda had long ago resigned herself to being noticed only because she was Hildy's friend. Now, with an effort, she looked back into Frank's laughing eyes and hoped her voice wouldn't give her away.

"I . . . I guess I'm just tired, that's all. I'm sorry —"

"But not too tired to help me study for that math test this afternoon," Hildy reminded her cheerfully. She wiggled in under Frank's arm and ran her lips lightly over his sleeve.

Belinda put a palm to her forehead and groaned. "Oh, Hildy, I forgot — Mrs. Thorne is supposed to pick me up to go meet Adam."

"How could you forget? You know I'm barely passing that class — you *always* help me study — and graduation's almost here and —"

Frank took up the plea in earnest as Belinda disentangled herself. "She'll flunk if you don't help her — and it'll be on *your* conscience." He gave Belinda a smug grin, and she sighed.

"What's wrong with *you* helping her for a

change? You're on the honor roll, too, you know. Student council. Math honor society — shall I go on?"

"But that's all instinct! You can't teach genius like mine! And anyway, I *do* help her study." Frank narrowed his eyes, focusing in on Hildy's too-tight sweater. "I help her study *lots* of things — explore new uncharted territories, go where no man has ever gone before. . . ."

Belinda didn't want to hear anymore. "Look, I'm going to try and get out of this interview, okay? But in case I can't, it shouldn't take that long. You can come over later —"

"Instead of being with me?" Frank stepped back, shocked. "*No* passing grade's worth that!"

"Then you'll just have to come with me," Hildy said sweetly. "I'm sure Belinda won't mind, will you, Belinda? And a little more intellectual stimulation certainly wouldn't hurt you."

"Come to think of it, *any* kind of stimulation certainly wouldn't hurt me." Frank ducked as Hildy swung at him, then he caught her arm and pulled her close for a kiss. Belinda sighed and hurried on ahead, but suddenly Frank yelled, "Look, Belinda — there goes your bus!"

Without even thinking, Belinda started to run. It wasn't until she was already at the corner and heard Frank laughing that she realized the bus wasn't even in sight yet.

"Frank, you are such a *jerk*." Hildy shook her head at him, but Belinda could tell she was trying not to laugh.

"Hey, is that any way to talk to the King of Fools? It was just a joke! Belinda knows it — *I* know it — you don't see *her* getting all bent out of shape —"

Hildy caught up with Belinda, glowering back at Frank over her shoulder. "So I'll see you tonight, okay?"

"Sure. That's fine."

"Belinda . . . are you mad at me?"

"Of course not. I told you, I'm just tired, that's all."

Hildy nodded, a slow frown creasing her brow. "I really think . . . I mean . . . you're really worrying way too much."

Belinda shrugged and tried to smile. "I guess so. You're probably right."

"And anyway," Frank added, falling into step beside them, "how *could* this guy's accident be the same one? You heard the explosion —"

"Frank, please," Hildy warned, but Frank bent low and peered hard into Belinda's face.

"You know I'm right, Belinda. That car blew sky-high. Nobody — *nobody* — could have survived it."

"Oh, look, there really *is* your bus —" Hildy gave her a little push. "See you later!"

With a wave, Belinda sprinted across the street and just managed to squeeze through the doors as the bus started off again. Finding an empty seat near the middle, she sank down and lowered her head to her books, her eyes closing wearily.

Nobody — nobody — could have survived it.

She felt tears stinging behind her eyelids and she

squeezed them back, only half conscious of the bumping and swaying of the bus, the drone of the motor, the squeal and swish of the doors as silent passengers got on and off. Frank was right, of course, there was no way anyone could have escaped that flaming, mangled mess . . . not anyone in that car . . . not that face trapped upside down, screaming for help . . . burning alive —

Rousing herself, Belinda suddenly realized she was at her stop and made an awkward dash out onto the curb. Her house was at the very end of the street, and she walked briskly, turning up her collar against the sharp breeze. It always felt so good to get home, to close the door behind her and just shut out the world for a while. She quickened her pace, a welcome feeling of relief creeping across her shoulders as she spied the familiar rooftop ahead.

And then she froze, books crushed to her chest.

A police car was parked in front of her house. Two uniformed men were strolling across the lawn while several neighborhood boys watched curiously. She felt her legs carrying her forward, propelling her down the sidewalk, across the yard and up the driveway.

"What is it?" she cried, and they were peering in through the windows, trying the handles on the doors. "What are you doing?"

A tall, swarthy policeman turned and came toward her, blocking her path. "Do you live here, miss?"

Belinda swallowed hard . . . nodded.

"Then you must know a Belinda Swanson?"

"I'm Belinda Swanson." She tried to go around him, but he sidestepped neatly into her path. "I live here. I live here in this house — what's wrong?"

His suspicious frown towered over her. "You wouldn't happen to know anything about a phone call, would you?"

"Phone call?" Her voice sounded as blank as she looked. From somewhere came the slow realization that the man was angry and that her stomach was churning.

"Someone called and told us you'd had some kind of accident," he challenged.

Sounds roared through her head like faraway echoes. The policeman's face swam back and then focused in again.

"Accident?" Her voice was faint.

"Do you have some form of identification?"

"My driver's license."

"Do you mind if we have a look around?"

"Of course not." She fumbled in her purse for her wallet and keys. The policeman's eyebrows were drawn down, eyes raking her over with a cold stare. He stood there with her while his partner went through the house. Belinda watched numbly, wondering how her legs were even holding her, until the other man finally reported back, shaking his head.

"Where are your parents now?"

"They're divorced. My mom's at work — she won't be home till later. . . ."

Her answer seemed to check him momentarily. He handed back her driver's license and nodded.

"Do you have any idea who might have called this in?"

"I . . . no."

Strangely enough, he seemed to believe her, for suddenly he stepped back, his voice a little kinder. "It sounded a little phony to me, but we have to check out every report. Kids don't realize how stupid these pranks can be. They — or you — could get in serious trouble."

"I'm sorry," Belinda mouthed, but she wasn't sure if the words came out loud enough for him to hear. She stood there forever . . . staring . . . thinking . . . and then the car was gone . . . and she stumbled blindly into her house.

Chapter 3

"Hello?"

"Hi, stranger. Think we'll ever get our schedules together again?"

"Oh, hi, Mom." Belinda sagged back against the kitchen counter, wrapping the phone cord around her arm, clinging to the warmth of her mother's voice.

"What is it, honey? You sound funny."

"Oh, nothing . . . I mean, I'm just tired."

"Rough day?"

"You could say that."

"Me, too. I'm low on nurses and overloaded with patients. Oh, and while I'm thinking of it, we got the weirdest phone call here this morning. I wasn't on the floor when it came, but someone named Thorne called and was asking questions about 'Miss Swanson.' Janet took the call — she said there were *two* Miss Swansons who worked here — meaning you and me — and —"

Belinda felt herself going cold. "Thorne? She called there?"

"Uh-huh . . . do you know who it was?"

"Well . . ." Belinda's heart sank. "It *must* have been Mrs. Thorne. I have a job interview with her today — she wants me to tutor her stepson."

"Hmmm. Why would she call here, I wonder? To get references?"

"I don't know. Maybe . . . well . . . her stepson was hurt . . . in some kind of accident, I think."

"Oh, honey, that's too bad. Maybe she wants to make sure you're qualified to work with someone who's injured."

"Well . . . that's kind of what I've been wondering about." Belinda forced her voice to sound casual, though her palm sweated against the receiver. "I'm just not sure I want to do it, you know?"

"But it sounds so perfect for you. And I thought you really liked tutoring —"

"I know, Mom, but — well — this guy's sick and I just don't know if I'd be good around him —"

"After all the volunteer work you've done these past years?" Mrs. Swanson's voice chided a little. "Honey, you're a natural with sick people. Or is this lifetime dream of nursing school suddenly being reconsidered?"

"Well . . . I . . ." Belinda shut her eyes, feeling trapped. "Of course not. I'm just . . ."

"Nervous." Mrs. Swanson chuckled, not unkindly. "Hey, that's natural, believe me, I don't care what job it is. Want my opinion?"

Belinda smiled in spite of herself. "Do I have a choice?"

"No." This time Mom laughed heartily. "Try it

out. Meet the young man. See how it goes between you two. You never know what might come of it."

"No," Belinda said, a stab in the pit of her stomach. "You never know."

"And that poor boy," Mom added sympathetically. "I wonder what kind of accident he had?"

"Uh, Mom, I have to go." Belinda forced down another wave of nausea and looked out the window as a horn sounded from the driveway. "Mrs. Thorne's here now to pick me up."

"I have to run, too — all hell's breaking loose down here! What can I say, huh? The emergency room can't manage without me!"

Belinda said good-bye and hung up the phone with a sad smile. *I can't manage without you, either, Mom. I'm doing a lousy job, and oh, by the way, did you know your daughter, the future Florence Nightingale, murdered someone about two weeks ago? Just a joke, Mom. . . .*

Mrs. Thorne gave a polite greeting as Belinda climbed into the Mercedes beside her, but she seemed even more strained since their last meeting. Several times she glanced over as if wanting to say something, then turned her eyes quickly back to the windshield. Belinda tried to fill the awkward silence by chatting about school and graduation, but when that didn't work, she gave up and simply gazed out at the wealthy neighborhoods as they drove through — the lush lawns and sprawling houses so different from those on her own street.

Frank. It had to have been Frank who played that trick on the police. The thought had been pounding at her ever since the two officers had left, and now she gave in to it angrily, even more angry at herself. Frank and Hildy had been trying to get through to her all this time, and maybe it was time she finally listened. This accident of Mrs. Thorne's couldn't have anything to do with April Fools' Day — coincidences like that were just too ridiculous — too *impossible*. She didn't want to think about what the policeman had said to her — *"they said you'd had some kind of accident"* — she didn't want to think about *any* kind of accident — she just wanted to stop worrying and get on with her life —

"Belinda, are you all right? You look a little upset."

Belinda jumped, her mouth struggling to smile. "No, I'm fine."

"You should have told me you get carsick — I surely would have gone slower."

"No, I never get carsick. I'm sorry . . . it must be 'cause I skipped lunch today."

"I'll have Cobbs fix you something when he gets home," Mrs. Thorne said.

"Who's Cobbs?"

"He's been with my husband's family for years." Mrs. Thorne waved one hand, diamonds sparkling on her fingers. "He keeps the household running smoothly; he knows how disruptions upset me. And Adam, God knows —" As she spoke his name, her mouth pressed into a hard line, and Belinda glanced at her questioningly. "Belinda," Mrs. Thorne said carefully, her eyes fixed on the road ahead, "perhaps I should warn you about Adam."

Belinda threw the woman a startled glance, receiving a grim smile in return.

"Am I making it sound ominous? It's very simple, really — he probably won't want you there. I feel I should prepare you for that."

Belinda nodded and waited for her to go on. Mrs. Thorne drew a deep breath, her hands tightening on the wheel.

"He's very hostile."

"You mean . . . dangerous?"

Her shrug was noncommittal. "He doesn't want to be helped. He won't trust you, I can promise you that."

"But you did tell him, didn't you? About me coming, I mean?"

The woman seemed not to have heard. "There have been . . . other problems . . . in the past. I'm sure it's obvious to you that we don't get along. Quite simply, I hate Adam and Adam hates me."

Belinda didn't know how to respond. The car slowed, turned through a remote-controlled gate onto a wide, flower-lined driveway, stopped alongside a magnificent house surrounded by low-sweeping trees and thick shrubbery. It was breathtaking, and yet Belinda sensed something missing, some feeling of warmth and personality. She stared at the brick and stone walls, the windows speckled with deep shade and leftover raindrops from that morning's shower. Mrs. Thorne patted a wisp of bleached blonde hair into place.

"My husband loves this house — it's not right that Adam's here and he's not. Adam should be in that hospital dying, not Fred. If it were up to me, I'd never see Adam again. And once his father dies, I won't have to." She switched off the motor, making no move to get out. "If he's angry or aloof, it has nothing to do with you."

"Is he in pain?" Belinda asked quietly.

Mrs. Thorne hesitated, and Belinda forced herself to ask the question she'd been most dreading to ask.

"How badly was he hurt?"

Again the woman shrugged. She looked impatient as she opened her door. "At least he doesn't need a nurse. That's one expense we don't have to fool with." Belinda looked at her, shocked, but she was already heading for the front door. "Come along. Just meet Adam for yourself."

But you don't understand, Belinda wanted to scream, I don't want to meet Adam — I don't even want to be here. She followed Mrs. Thorne into the house, her heart fluttering. Just a coincidence, Hildy and Frank had said. Nothing to worry about. *And they must know what they're talking about because this place looks so normal and so safe. . . .*

"Your house is beautiful," Belinda said politely, taking in the entryway, the living room beyond. There were flowers and figurines on shelves, and on all the tables and countertops there were strange box-shaped objects draped with cloths. Belinda stared at them, wondering what they were, but Mrs. Thorne was already getting out of her coat and nodding toward a curving staircase that led to a balcony above. Belinda saw an open hallway there, and a row of solidly shut doors. The house was absolutely still.

"You can leave your things on the couch." Mrs. Thorne started up the stairs and motioned Belinda to follow. "Adam's room is up here."

"Maybe you should just tell him I'm —" Belinda's voice shook, but Mrs. Thorne wasn't listening. She continued up the steps and down the hallway, and when she finally stopped at the last door, her knock echoed coldly down the long corridor.

"Adam," she said, "I've brought someone to meet you."

There was an answer from within that Belinda couldn't quite hear. A muffled voice that caused Mrs. Thorne to pull back and look uncertainly at the door.

"Maybe I should leave," Belinda began, but suddenly she was being pulled forward and the door was being opened, and she stumbled into a dim confusion of half-light and silence.

"This is Belinda," Mrs. Thorne said.

And then Belinda heard the door close . . . the sound of feet moving quickly back down the stairs. . .

And the soft, slow shifting of someone who watched her from the shadows.

Chapter 4

It seemed an eternity that she stood there, her eyes struggling to adjust to the gloom. In her panic she saw the dull outline of a shaded window . . . the crouching shapes of furniture . . . and finally, frighteningly . . . a vague silhouette standing in the farthest, darkest corner. Fighting down an overwhelming urge to run, Belinda spoke into the shadows.

"Adam? I'm . . . I'm Belinda —"

"I know who you are," the voice said. It was deep and expressionless, but very soft, and Belinda's heart caught in her throat.

"You know —"

"She told me you'd be coming."

Weakness washed over her in a great wave. "Oh. I . . . I wasn't sure she had."

"You're wasting your time," the voice said. "I don't need any help. With studying or anything else."

Belinda nodded, relief making her braver. "But your . . . Mrs. Thorne . . . wants me here. And since I'm already here, couldn't we just get acquainted?" She waited for a reply, but nothing came. "We don't have to do any studying today, you know. We could just talk and —"

"I don't have anything to say to you."

"All right. Then *I'll* talk." She took a hesitant step forward. "If you decide you don't like me, then I won't come back."

"And what if you decide you don't like *me?*" the voice fired back.

"Well . . . I . . . I can't think of any reason why I —"

"Your voice is shaking," Adam said. "What are you afraid of?"

Belinda froze. "You," she said quietly. She was shocked that she'd admitted it, shocked that she would give him such an advantage. For a long, long moment there was silence. When he finally made a sound in his throat, she couldn't tell if it was a sigh . . . or a laugh."

"How perceptive," Adam said. "Especially when you haven't even seen me yet."

Belinda chose her words carefully. "But I'd like to see you. Maybe you could turn on the light . . ."

"I prefer it dark. Believe me, you'll prefer it, too."

"I might not." Yet even as she said it, Belinda's mind swirled with the horrible possibilities that she'd tried so hard to suppress — *that face . . . trapped upside down . . . burning. . . .* "I've worked at hospitals." Again she surprised herself, calm words welling up from the depths of her fear. "I've seen lots of things before, so I doubt very much that you could shock me."

She paused, but he didn't answer. Around her the threatening shapes had begun to resume their everyday ordinariness. A bed. A chest of drawers. A desk and chair. But still, back in the corner beyond the darkened window, an invisible face hid among the shadows.

"Mrs. Thorne said you don't usually live here," she tried again, took another step forward. "Do you come here a lot? For visits, I mean?" She wracked her brain, words tumbling out in a nervous rush. "How long have you been here this time?" Her ears strained through the silence, finally catching his belligerent reply.

"A week."

"Oh. A week. Well, then, you've had some time to settle —"

"Look, you're wasting your time and mine. My dear stepmother feels . . . shall we say, *obligation* — to my dying father? That's all. She's just using you to ease her own conscience. It's got nothing to do with me or my welfare."

"My mother's never home, either. She works all the time because we need the money, and she's never there when I really need to talk to her. But I still know she loves me." Again Belinda stopped, startled at her own confession. She'd never said that to anyone before — not to Mom — not to Hildy — not even to herself. She must be crazy, talking like this to some total stranger who didn't give a damn about her or —

"Aren't you lucky." It was a sarcastic remark, but the tone was almost sad as it hung there in the darkness between them. There was a slight rustling as if he had moved, and Belinda stepped back, ready to flee. "Relax," Adam said. "I couldn't move that fast, even if I wanted to."

And then, as Belinda stared in disbelief, the figure by the window began to come toward her.

It gathered itself from the shadows like smoke, and as it pulled slowly and purposefully across the floor, Belinda was suddenly aware of two things:

He was using a cane.

And one of his feet dragged uselessly behind the other.

Adam stopped near the desk, his breathing slow and even in the room's quietness. Belinda stood still, knowing he watched her. She could feel his anger in the air, so real and so incredibly strong. Her heart ached, not only for him, but for herself and her awful uncertainties.

"I'm . . . I'm so sorry about your accident —
I —"

"Are you, Belinda?" Adam sounded amused. "Are you so sorry that it keeps you awake nights?"

That sick feeling again, rising up into her throat. Belinda forced it back, her voice weak. "Do you . . . do you want to talk about what happened?"

The room was so hot — so suddenly and unbearably hot — and in a kind of slow haze she saw her hands out in front of her, searching for something to hold on to.

"Do you . . ." she tried again, but the darkness

was growing even blacker, and the room was turning upside down — "Adam," she gasped, and there was nothing to break her fall, no one to help her as she slumped down onto the floor — just thick blackness and a muffled roar in her ears, and suddenly, frighteningly, a hunched shape leaning over her.

Memories drowned her, dozens of them in such short seconds, and as Belinda struggled back to full consciousness, she felt hands gripping her arms, amazingly strong, calm hands beneath her shoulders. From some vague distance she thought someone spoke her name, but as her eyelids fluttered open there was only the silence . . . and shadows. . . .

And the thing looking down at her.

For a split second she thought she'd passed out again, that her faint had turned into some cruel, hideous nightmare.

And then she realized he was real.

In the eerie half-light she saw part of his face, the eyes so dark they seemed like holes in a death mask. There were huge gashes — black, crooked lines crisscrossing his cheeks and forehead like jagged tracks, and as her eyes widened in horror, he suddenly released her and drew back into the cover of darkness.

Belinda lay there, not moving. The ceiling stopped swirling, the room righted itself, settled calmly back around her.

Several feet away, Adam was as silent as stone.

Belinda raised herself slowly on her elbows, trembling with a million emotions. "Adam," she said softly, "why don't you come back out."

"If you're better, I wish you'd just leave." He sounded drained, yet beneath the emptiness Belinda thought his voice quivered.

"I don't think I can get up yet. I might fall down again." He didn't answer so she rushed on, her voice still unsteady. "It's because I haven't eaten anything — I just got so hot all of a sudden — I haven't really felt very good all day and —"

"You said I couldn't shock you, but you were wrong."

Belinda shook her head, willing him to believe her. "No, that's not true. It's just that I passed out for a second and I didn't know where I was. It scared me, that's all. I'm sorry if I upset you —"

"Please," he murmured, "just go."

She stared unhappily in the direction of his voice. She felt embarrassed and light-headed, but even worse she felt like she'd let him down. Getting slowly to her feet, she paused in the threshold, light from the hallway falling just short of his hiding place. "Good-bye, Adam. I'll see you tomorrow, okay?"

There was no answer. She couldn't even pick out his shadow from the others.

It seemed strange to be out in the brightness again. As Belinda went slowly down the stairs, she squinted against creamy walls and pastel colors, her eyes going automatically to the cloth-draped boxes around the room. They looked like different-sized blocks of some kind — cages or aquariums all covered with dark scarves and again she wondered what they could possibly be. *Some weird sort of art? Sculpture?* There didn't seem to be anyone around, and she wanted to get home. She stood uncertainly in the middle of the room and listened for a moment, hearing only deep, stark silence.

"Mrs. Thorne?" she called softly.

Her voice faded, unacknowledged, and she shivered at its lonely sound.

"Mrs. Thorne, are you here? I'm ready to go home now."

Belinda frowned and walked slowly about the room, looking for a clock. She had her own homework to do before Hildy came over, and there was no telling how long the studying would take if Frank came, too. If there was one distraction Hildy didn't need tonight, it was Frank.

"Mrs. Thorne?" Belinda called again. She stopped beside a coffee table and leaned closer to inspect the fabric-covered box on top of it. And then she frowned and pulled back. Just now . . . she thought she'd heard a noise from inside. A soft . . . soft . . . rustling . . .

Cautiously she reached out to touch the cloth . . . to lift one corner away.

She hadn't heard anyone slip into the room behind her.

She didn't even see the hand as it came out of nowhere and clamped down on her wrist.

"I wouldn't do that if I were you," the voice said.

With a scream, Belinda jumped back.

The man towered over her, gaunt and expressionless, his hooded eyes fixed calmly on her face.

41

And as Belinda stared up at him, she noticed the slight movement of his other arm . . . his smooth attempt to hide something behind his back . . . something shiny . . . yet smeared with dull red. . . .

A meat cleaver.

Chapter 5

"I wouldn't do that if I were you, miss," he said again. "Some of them are quite dangerous. Hardly safe to touch." He lifted the cloth, and Belinda's eyes widened. A screen was fastened on top of the box, and there below it, coiled in the bottom, was a thick brown snake. "A hobby of Mr. Thorne's. Revolting, really."

Belinda couldn't stop shaking. She looked back at him as he replaced the cloth, not knowing whether to laugh or to cry, and then she pointed weakly toward his back.

"Oh, this?" He gave the cleaver a disinterested glance. "I was just preparing dinner. Didn't want to frighten you."

Belinda's voice wavered. "You . . . you must be Mr. Cobbs?"

"Cobbs, miss, yes. And you're no doubt Miss Belinda."

She nodded, still studying him. He was well over six feet tall, ramrod straight and very thin, with a cadaverous sort of face and pale, calm eyes, which had remained half-closed throughout their conversation. He was dressed in a black suit, starched and neat, and Belinda doubted if he ever so much as wrinkled when he moved. It was hard to tell exactly how old he was — with that angular face and receding white hairline; she guessed that Cobbs had been born looking like an old man. And then, as she continued her scrutiny, it occurred to her that he knew exactly what she was doing, and she dropped her eyes in embarrassment.

"I was looking for Mrs. Thorne," she said quickly.

"Logical choice of locations."

"I really need to get home."

"Come with me."

Cobbs had that kind of voice that left no room for argument, and Belinda followed him into a gigantic, gleaming kitchen.

"Sit there." Cobbs nodded at a spotless tile bar that separated the cooking area from a smaller breakfast room.

"But I have to get —"

"Sit down, miss. I'll fix you some tea and toast, and then I'll take you home. If you'll forgive my saying so, you look a trifle . . . anxious."

Belinda gave a grim smile and hoisted herself onto a high stool at the counter. She propped her chin in her hands and watched as Cobbs put the kettle on the stove, rinsed a flowered teapot with hot water, and measured tea from a blue cannister. He moved quickly without hurrying, and Belinda had the feeling he could find his way around this kitchen in his sleep.

"Sugar?" he glanced at her. "Cream?"

"I've never had cream in my tea," Belinda said doubtfully.

Cobbs lowered his head, but Belinda could almost swear he'd rolled his eyes. "It's the civilized thing to do, miss."

"Oh. Then I guess I'd better try it —"

"Splendid." He crossed to an oaken china cupboard on a wall in the breakfast room and took down a delicate cup and saucer, which he placed before her.

"Aren't you having some, too?" Belinda asked.

"I, miss?"

"Yes. I'd feel better if you'd have some, too."

A tiny flicker of — what? shock? amusement? — showed in his eyes. He regarded her thoughtfully, then fetched another cup and saucer.

"I just . . . well . . . you really don't have to treat me like company, you know," Belinda said uncomfortably. "I'm not used to being waited on."

"Obviously." He filled the teapot, and waited for it to steep. When it was ready, he filled Belinda's cup and returned to the stove.

Belinda pointed to the stool beside her. "Don't you want to sit down?"

"If it makes you more comfortable."

"Yes, it would." Belinda watched, relieved, as he perched himself on the edge of the stool. He looked like a strange, exotic bird very much out of his element. "Maybe we should sit at the table," she said.

"Excellent idea."

Together they took their cups and a plate of toast and sat across from each other — after Cobbs had pulled out her chair and seated her. The tea tasted wonderful, and with the first few sips, Belinda smiled hesitantly and leaned back in her chair.

"This is really good. I like it."

"That certainly makes my day."

"You're from England, aren't you?"

"What was your first clue?"

Belinda's smile widened. "Your accent, of course. And you're very . . . stiff."

Cobbs conceded with a nod.

"So how did you end up here? Mrs. Thorne says you've been with the family for a long time."

Another nod. "My father worked for Mr. Thorne's grandfather. We go back many years."

Belinda hesitated, wanting to know . . . not sure she should ask. "Is Mr. Thorne really . . . dying?"

"He's in a coma. He knows no one. His body was severely crushed and burned. It's merely a matter of time."

"I'm so sorry," Belinda mumbled, and hurried to change the subject. "I've always wanted to go to England. Do you miss it?"

"I left when I was quite a young man. I've spent more of my life in this country now than the other."

Belinda sipped thoughtfully at her tea, the warmth seeping through her body, sweet and relaxing. She could almost imagine that she'd never seen that cage in the other room. "Why are there snakes in the house?"

"It's Mr. Thorne's wishes. Eccentric, perhaps, but law."

"But . . . aren't you afraid they'll get out?"

Across from her the old man's face remained bland. "I live in terror."

She shifted her eyes away as he caught her staring again, and her glance lighted on two gold-framed photographs arranged side by side on a windowsill. They were both boys she was sure she didn't know, and yet one of them seemed unsettlingly familiar.

"Mr. Cobbs —"

"Just Cobbs, miss."

Belinda nodded. "Those pictures over there — who are they?"

"Why, the sons, of course."

"Sons?"

"Dear little darlings of the household." He raised one shaggy eyebrow. "Mister Noel and Mister Adam."

"Oh! Then that one on the left —"

"Yes, miss. You met him upstairs. That's Mister Adam. Mr. Thorne's son from his first marriage. Noel belongs to the Madame."

"May I look?"

Cobbs shrugged, and she crossed to the window, picking up each frame in turn. The boy called Noel was standing on a beach, his hair all windblown and sun-bleached, his eyes soft and hazel-colored, and there was a huge dog at his side. But Adam . . .

Something caught in Belinda's throat as she gazed at the darkness of Adam. Defiance showed in every unsmiling line of his face — his ruggedly handsome face — not the face that had frightened her so upstairs. His eyes and hair were raven black, his face tanned like Noel's, but more naturally, not just from the seasonal rays of the sun. He looked beautiful and evil at the same time, and Belinda felt tears filling her eyes.

He was standing at the edge of a cliff, and he was straight and tall and unscarred —

"Do you know anything about his accident?" Belinda's voice trembled, and she ran one finger over the smooth glass of Adam's cheek.

"He doesn't talk about it. It's not my place to ask." Behind her she heard Cobbs get up from the table, and she hastily wiped her eyes. She turned and he was looking at her, but then he looked away, busying himself at the counter, chopping with his cleaver.

"Do you . . . do you happen to know how Mrs. Thorne got my name?" she asked quietly.

"I only saw a small card advertising your services. I assume she saw it posted somewhere."

Belinda glanced over at him and replaced the picture on the sill. "Adam wouldn't let me see him," she said softly. "It was . . . scary."

The cleaver paused in midair . . . lowered noiselessly to the countertop. "Some scars run deeper than those we can see."

Puzzled, she turned and stared at his rigid back. "Mrs. Thorne doesn't want him, does she?"

A long pause, and then, "Not if she can possibly avoid it."

And Belinda nodded, although there was no one

to see her except the unsmiling face of Adam as she tilted him carefully into the light. "Then maybe I'll take this job, Mr. Cobbs."

The cleaver lifted slowly, came down again with a wet thud on the raw meat.

"If you're ready, I'll drive you home now."

That strong, challenging face . . . full of dark secrets and dark emotions . . . With a sigh Belinda closed her Spanish book, realizing she had no idea what she'd just read. *Adam Thorne, whatever happened to you, couldn't have anything to do with me . . . but I'm going to help you come out of your darkness.* She sighed again as she heard a car in the driveway. Frank and Hildy were already here. She couldn't remember when she'd ever felt less like seeing them.

"So?" Hildy burst through the back door, flinging her coat onto the kitchen table. "Did you take the job? I want to hear all about it — don't leave anything out —"

"Is this gonna take very long?" Frank opened the refrigerator door and helped himself to a Pepsi, then rummaged for something to eat. "Hey, your cupboard's kinda bare, Belinda. Hurry up with the lessons, will you? There's a movie we wanna catch. And maybe — if Hildy's a *real* good girl — a nice surprise after that."

Hildy looked intrigued. "What kind of surprise? Where are we going?"

"I was thinking . . . maybe a little action. You know — up at Suicide Drop."

Belinda shuddered. "You don't *really* take Hildy up there, do you?"

"What's the matter with that? It's nice and deserted . . . dark and quiet . . . perfect for making out — wish it was *you* I was taking instead?" Frank grinned.

Hildy shook her head at Belinda. "Don't worry. He's always trying to get me to go up there with him, but wild horses couldn't drag me. Yuck . . . just thinking of that awful place gives me' the creeps. Frank, sometimes I think you're totally insane."

"No, you think I'm totally irresistible. And where's your sense of adventure? Your sense of romance?"

"You mean her sense of intelligence," Belinda frowned. "And anyway, that road's been closed for months."

"The better to be alone together, my dear," Frank gave a wicked chuckle, and Belinda turned away, trying to shut the whole idea out of her head.

Everyone knew about Suicide Drop, the hill outside of town that had claimed so many innocent lives. Its narrow dirt road descended almost straight down, then cut sharply between a jagged slope on one side, and a sheer drop to rocks below on the other. Its danger was also deceiving — most people didn't even realize how quickly their car could pick up speed until they were too close to the cliff to make the curve. Thinking about it now reminded Belinda of the road near the airport, and she nearly dropped the coffeepot she was filling.

"So what do you think?" Frank asked again. "An hour? Two at the most? How long is all this stupid homework gonna take?"

"That depends on Hildy," Belinda said shortly, and Frank spun around with a grin.

"My, my, aren't we touchy tonight! What happened — you get canned today before you even started your job?"

"Frank," Hildy gave him a warning look and he shrugged, finally settling on a jar of olives, which he took to the table. "Okay, Belinda," Hildy turned back, "what happened? We were right, weren't we? You did all that worrying for nothing." She gave a triumphant grin, but it faded at the look on her friend's face.

"I don't know," Belinda said.

"What do you mean, you don't know?" Frank snorted. "It's either a coincidence or *you're* crazy. Very simple." Hildy glared at him and he promptly popped an olive into each eye and made a face at her.

"Stop it, Frank; that's disgusting." Hildy pulled her chair close to Belinda. "So why don't you know?"

"He won't talk about his accident. He won't even let me see his face." She shuddered inwardly, remembering that distorted image in the dark. "He's all stitched up and something's wrong with his legs — he uses a cane. I don't know. . . . I just don't want to believe we could have caused something like that. . . ."

For a split second Hildy's expression fell, and she looked confused. It was Frank who leaned forward, his voice so self-assured in the sudden, uncomfortable quiet.

"Just cut it out, huh, Belinda? *You* know and *I* know and *Hildy* knows — in our *heart* of *hearts* — that it's absolutely *impossible* for —"

"Nothing's impossible, Frank," Belinda said firmly. He looked a little surprised, but still shook his head at her.

"Talk about a guilty conscience! Jeez, it's just gonna eat and eat at you —"

"You should have heard the way Adam talked," Belinda shook her head. "Things he said to me — almost as if he *knows* me, it's creepy —"

"You are so *easy* to scare." Frank chuckled. "*Anybody* could scare you —"

"Let's study," Hildy said hurriedly. "Let's get this over with so we can see the movie. You, too, Belinda, you come, too —"

"No." Her voice was tight. "I don't feel like a movie."

"You'll excuse me then if I miss this *fascinating* discussion." Frank stood up, his mouth full, and took his snacks with him into the living room. "I need some — what was that, Hildy? Intellectual stimulation. In front of the TV. Hey, where's your paper?"

Belinda pressed her lips together. "Outside, I guess. I forgot to bring it in."

Hildy stared down at the table as Belinda opened her math book, laid out her notes, set out paper and pencils between them. "Belinda . . . really . . . why don't you come with us? It'll be good for you to get out —"

"No, I don't want to." She sat down in the chair, then lowered her head in her hands.

"Belinda — what is it?"

"You should have see him, Hildy. Before the accident, I mean."

"Before? But how — ?"

"I saw a picture of him and he was so gorgeous . . . tall, dark, and handsome —"

"Just your type," Hildy teased, but her smile was sincere. "I told you, didn't I tell you? That this could be *him?* Mr. Right?"

"Oh, Hildy." Belinda's voice faded. She felt Hildy's hand on her arm. "If Adam really *was* in that accident, I'll never forgive myself."

"So is that why you're taking the job?"

"I don't know. I've *got* to find out for sure, but I really want to *help* him, too — I just don't know. He . . . he scares me. And they keep *snakes* in the house."

"Oh, *gross!* How *weird!* Look, I wish you'd just forget about everything once and for all. I just wish you'd —"

"Hey, Belinda" — Frank reappeared in the doorway, examining something in his hands — "there was a package on your porch."

"A package?" Belinda took the small box he held out to her and shook it. Nothing rattled inside. Her own name was scrawled sloppily across the brown wrapping, but there was no return address.

"What do you think it is?" Hildy took it from her and shook it again, frowning. "There're no stamps, no forms. Someone must have left it."

"Who?" Belinda looked blank. "I don't know anyone who'd have left me anything."

"Uh-oh" — Frank shook his finger at her — "you're holding out on us, Belinda. Some secret admirer you're not telling us about."

Belinda ignored him and ripped the paper at one end of the box. The cardboard underneath was unmarked. She eased the wrapping off carefully, looking for any clue that might be below, but there was nothing. Just a small, flat, ordinary box.

She looked up at Hildy. Hildy looked at Frank.

"You open it," Belinda said suddenly, thrusting the box at Frank. For a second he looked startled, but then he laughed.

"Okay, but if it's something personal, don't blame me." He slid his finger under each taped end, then slowly lifted the lid.

Belinda's hand gripped the edge of the table.

Frank stared a moment, then began to chuckle. "It's a piece of paper." He held the folded object up between his fingers, and Hildy gave a nervous laugh. "Okay, Belinda, satisfied?" Frank shook his head. "Now *you* read it. It'd probably embarrass me."

Belinda took the paper, relief flooding through her. *What did you think it would be, anyway? You're so silly.* Yet she'd had a terrible feeling that it would be *something* . . . something *bad* . . . and now that it wasn't, she felt almost giddy.

"Go on, what's it say?" Hildy nudged her.

Belinda unfolded the paper, smiling at her own foolishness.

And then the smile froze on her lips.

"What is it?" Hildy was watching her, and suddenly none of it was funny anymore.

"It's . . . it's a calender," Belinda whispered.

"A what?"

"A . . . a page from a calendar. April." Belinda let the paper flutter from her fingers. "Oh, God —"

"What *is* it?" Hildy's voice was shrill, and Frank snatched up the page as Belinda sagged back in her chair.

"What is that, Frank?" she asked tonelessly. And he stared at her, not answering, his face suddenly unsure. "That mark, Frank — that mark on the first of April — Frank, *what is that?*"

And his mouth moved, but nothing came out, and Belinda shut her eyes and said it again.

"That circle around April Fools' Day, Frank — April Fools' Day —"

"It couldn't be," Frank said quietly. "It looks like . . . like dried blood."

Chapter 6

Someone knows . . . someone knows . . . someone —

"Hey, Belinda, wait up!"

Belinda spun around, startled, as Hildy came running across the schoolyard, braids streaming behind her in the playful wind.

"Didn't you hear me? I've been yelling and yelling!" Hildy stopped to catch her breath, trying to balance her books while she struggled into her sweater. Belinda looked on and said nothing. "I thought I'd *never* get out of there — dumb old Miss Cooper was lecturing us all on how dumb *we* are —"

"What about your math test?" Belinda broke into the nervous chatter, receiving only a shrug in response. "Oh, Hildy, you didn't —"

"Hey, it wasn't just me — the whole class flunked! And anyway, it wasn't your fault," Hildy said quickly. She finished zipping her front and flashed a carefree smile. "Belinda, come on, it's only a grade!"

"You haven't graduated yet, you know."

"I know, I know," Hildy mumbled. She shifted her books to her other arm, and the two girls started slowly toward the street. "Anyway, after what happened last night, who could study, huh?" Her glance slid sideways, her voice shaking a little. "Frank swears he didn't do it, but I think maybe he's joking."

Belinda felt a painful weight tightening in her chest. She hadn't slept a wink all night, and school had gone by in a blur. "Of course you do. It'd be too scary *not* to."

"But it *has* to be Frank. I mean . . . who *else* could it possibly be?" Hildy looked so intently into Belinda's eyes that Belinda looked away.

"The police were at my house yesterday," she said softly.

Hildy stopped and stared at her.

"Someone called in and said I'd had an accident."

Hildy looked skeptical. "Are you sure they had the right name? Maybe somebody got the message wrong."

"They said my name. And they were really suspicious, too — I could tell they thought something was going on. God, I was scared —"

"Oh, Belinda —" Hildy shook her head chidingly. "It was probably just someone —"

"Someone who? Someone Frank? Or someone who left their footprints up on the hill that night . . . and finally went to the cops?" Belinda walked away, leaving Hildy to stare after her, open-mouthed.

"Belinda! Hey, wait a minute —"

"I have to go." Belinda saw her bus coming and raced to the opposite corner.

"But I need to talk to you! About the senior picnic!" Hildy's voice followed her, but Belinda pretended not to hear.

Finding a seat, she closed her eyes, reliving the terror of last night — Hildy's pale face and accusations — Frank's denials. "Hey, you two, come on! April Fools' Day is *over*, remember?" He'd laughed at them and teased them all evening, but for the first time Belinda could tell it had shaken Hildy up.

Now she felt the bus slow down and she got off to transfer. Cobbs had told her he'd pick her up this afternoon, but she didn't want to have to depend on anyone. Also, this gave her the option of leaving whenever she chose. When she reached her final stop she realized that the swank neighborhood where the Thornes lived lay just on the other side of the park. She hadn't been to the park since last summer, but she knew her way around well. With its picnic grounds, its public gardens, and small amusement park area, it had been a frequent holiday treat when she was growing up, when Mom and Dad were happy and they were a real family. . . .

Forcing that thought away, Belinda started off, taking the main route through the gardens. The landscape design had changed through the years, old brick walkways now going nowhere, wandering in perpetual circles. As pathways had eventually fallen into disrepair and closed, older areas of the park had also been barricaded and shut off, yet she still remembered the shortcuts and used them when there was no one around to see. Slipping through a hole in one of the fences, she cut across an old, abandoned parking lot, now a graveyard for junked cars and outdated parts of mechanical rides. From this spot, she could hardly hear any park activity at all — it was like being in some alien world, surrounded by hulking metal monstrosities.

A windblown leaf scraped across the pavement, and she jumped. She glanced back over her shoulder, suddenly uneasy. Overhead the sun struggled weakly through a restless veil of clouds, and the afternoon was chilly. Winter had lingered late and gusty this year, with frost still falling at night. She buried her chin into the collar of her jacket and rammed her fists into her pockets, her fingers closing unexpectedly around a thick wad of cloth. Puzzled, she pulled it out and began stretching it apart, trying to remember where it had come from. Somehow it had gone unnoticed through the wash all balled up in her pocket.

And then she remembered.

This was the jacket she'd been wearing the night of the accident.

She'd been so wet and muddy that she'd washed all her clothes at Hildy's that very night. She must have forgotten about the rag she'd picked up, the rag she'd held to her bleeding face. This was the first time she'd even worn that jacket since then.

There were still bloodstains on the rag. Except now she could see that it wasn't really a rag at all, but a handkerchief, torn at one corner, right through an embroidered A.

Belinda shoved the thing back into her pocket and zipped her jacket up tighter against the chill, hurrying the last few yards to another high fence, letting herself back into the mainstream of the park. She was relieved when she saw her exit just ahead; the house was easy to find from there. She pressed the intercom buzzer on the gate and identified herself to a bored-sounding Cobbs, who was holding the front door open for her when she reached it. As soon as she stepped inside, Belinda heard Mrs. Thorne's voice in the living room.

"Oh, Belinda. You came back, that's good." The woman greeted her as if she really couldn't have cared less. "Adam's hiding, as usual. Go on up." She glanced in annoyance toward the balcony, then gestured at Cobbs. "My nerves, Cobbs — my nerves are going. Be sure and pack all my pills. And help me find something to wear. I have to catch that ungodly little commuter flight in less than three hours — I don't have any idea what to wear —"

"How about a gag, madame?"

"What about my bag? How should *I* know where the bags are, Cobbs? That's *your* job!"

"Is there anything I can do, Mrs. Thorne?" Belinda asked, but the woman brushed past her up the stairs.

"A business trip, Belinda," she said crisply. "I don't know how long I'll be gone. I shouldn't go, of course — I know I shouldn't go. Fred's lying there in the hospital, and what will people say? But it *is* his company, after all, and they'll do all they can to take advantage of him now."

Belinda couldn't believe what she was hearing. Cobbs seemed unperturbed.

"Take my advice, Belinda, and think twice before you marry for money — *or* convenience. It gets harder and harder to keep up appearances, and someone's always waiting for you to slip up . . . make a stupid mistake." She pulled a cigarette from the pocket of her robe and tossed it away again impatiently. "But what can I do?" She looked at Cobbs, annoyed. "What can I do, I ask you? Fred doesn't even know me. I can't do anything for Fred."

"No, madame."

"If I stay, I'll go crazy."

"Yes, madame."

"Between Fred and Adam, I'll just go out of my mind, won't I, Cobbs?"

"Right into the straitjacket, madame."

"So the best thing I can do for Fred is to stay away and leave him in peace, right, Cobbs?"

"I'm sure of *that*, madame."

"New York this time, can you believe that?" Mrs. Thorne looked angrily at Belinda. "I was *only* there last month — why can't they have problems somewhere else for a change?"

Belinda stared at her, dismayed. "But what about Adam?"

Mrs. Thorne paused on the top step, her face confused. "What *about* Adam?"

"Well . . ." Belinda looked back at Cobbs, who remained expressionless. "I mean . . . with the accident and everything —"

"*I* didn't ask him to come here, did I?" she said coolly. "He's not my responsibility. I'm sure you and Cobbs can handle his needs." Her eyes narrowed on Belinda disapprovingly. "If he was really important to anyone around here, his father would have had him come while he was still alive enough to enjoy him."

The door slammed behind her, and Belinda realized she'd been gripping the bannister so hard that her hand hurt. She felt a lump in her throat and looked furiously at Cobbs, who was inspecting a tabletop for dust.

"How could she say that?" Belinda asked tightly. "How can she be so — *heartless!* Doesn't she care about *anyone?*"

"Yes," Cobbs nodded. "Mrs. Thorne."

"I know Adam heard her, he couldn't help but hear all that —"

"The Statue of Liberty herself couldn't help but hear all that," Cobbs said, giving the table a quick dab with the end of his sleeve. "Perhaps you should go up, miss."

"Does Adam know I'm coming?"

"He'll be overjoyed, no doubt."

Belinda sighed and made her way to Adam's room. When her knock brought no response, she put her mouth close to the door. "Adam? It's Belinda. Are you ready to study?"

No answer.

Belinda turned the knob and peeked in. Total darkness just like before . . . the silhouette by the window. She could feel his belligerence even from here, and it touched her with sudden cold. Again she recalled the photograph on the windowsill, the handsome face, the daring expression. . . . *Me against the world*, it had said. And she knew that he had heard his stepmother's comments outside and something told her that he had heard comments just like them all his life, that he had grown used to them and now expected them —

"We don't have to study today if you don't want to. We can just talk. About anything you want —"

The silence went on and on. She knew they were in a contest of wills, and her sympathy battled with her determination. *It's obvious he doesn't want you here, so why don't you just go and spare yourself all this hassle — you don't need this right now, and Adam certainly doesn't need you, and you're just upsetting him, and what possible good can it do anyone —*

Someone knocked on the door behind her, and Belinda nearly jumped out of her skin. Cobbs came into the room without hesitation and set something down on the table.

"I don't want it." Adam sounded surly.

"I'm sure you don't," Cobbs replied. "God forbid you should take anything to improve your disposition." He turned and left the room again, and Belinda stifled the urge to call him back.

There was a slow scraping from the corner, as if something were uncoiling. Belinda thought of the snakes downstairs and shivered.

"So," Adam Thorne said, "you want to talk."

"Only if you do."

"About anything I want?" His voice was mocking, smooth, wrapping around her like an invisible web. "Then . . . I choose you."

"Me?" Belinda glanced self-consciously toward the shadows. "Oh, I don't think that'd be very interesting. I'd rather — "

"You said 'anything.' Why shouldn't it be you?"

Belinda's heart fluttered in her throat. "Well . . . all right then. What would you like to know?"

There was a long, thoughtful silence. Then, "Secrets," Adam said at last. "Everyone has them. Deep, dark ones way down inside."

"Secrets?" She forced out the words in a shaky rush. "But it wouldn't be fair, would it? For me to tell you my secrets if you didn't tell me yours?"

There was a sudden clinking of glass, as if something had overturned. Belinda started forward, then stopped herself as Adam cursed.

"Are you all right?" she asked carefully.

He sounded irritated. "Yes. Don't come any closer."

Belinda sighed, grateful for the distraction. "Is that medicine that Cobbs brings you? Are you in a lot of pain?"

The pause was wary. "Sometimes."

"Your legs?"

There was a soft sound; she imagined him shrugging at her, feeling trapped and hostile there in the dark because she wouldn't go away.

"Yes," he said finally.

She nodded, her voice unnaturally light. "I fell off a ladder once. I didn't think I'd hurt myself, but the next day I was so bruised and sore I could hardly move. I can't imagine how you'd feel after . . ." she forced out the words, "an accident."

He didn't answer so she eased herself down onto the floor, her back against the wall.

"I looked over your lesson plans with my principal at school. He said you could still graduate — that you can take exams late and it probably wouldn't be that hard for you to catch up on what you've missed. He's talked to your school — he said people there had been asking about you — did your stepmother tell you?"

"Of course," Adam said sarcastically. "Surely you couldn't have missed that affectionate display a minute ago."

Sympathetic anger bubbled up and Belinda nearly choked on it. "She probably doesn't even realize what she said — she's probably just so upset about your father —"

"One thing you have to remember about dear old Gloria," Adam said. "When my father dies, she'll be a very rich widow."

"Well . . . I . . . I thought maybe we could decide on some kind of schedule today . . . how often you'd like me to come. I don't want to tire you out or get in the way so —"

"Get in the way?" he suppressed a harsh laugh. "Of what? My busy social life?"

"Well . . . I only meant — "

"I know what you meant; I don't need your pity. I've been shoved off on you because they don't know what else to do with me, that's all."

"Oh, Adam, I'm sure that's not true, I —"

"I didn't ask to be here. I was sent. Because Mom didn't know 'how to deal with me.' I think that's the way she put it."

"But I heard she was really worried about you . . . that she thought a change of scene would be good for you."

"Good for me?" Adam echoed derisively. "God, it's so funny, isn't it?"

"What is?"

"How all the people who don't even *know* me are suddenly such experts on what's good for me." He seemed to be considering this, and Belinda spoke up timidly.

"I'm sure they're only trying to help."

"Help?" The deep voice mocked her. "Now, that's an interesting thought. And what about you, Belinda Swanson? Who are *you* trying to help?"

A cold, slow chill crawled over her as he gave a deep laugh in his throat. She sat there in the darkness, pinned against the wall by eyes she couldn't see . . . rising to her feet . . . feeling behind her for the door.

"Where are you going? You just got here."

"I have to get home. I — forgot I have something to do —"

The voice sounded coldly amused. "Uh-oh . . . was it something I said?"

Belinda stumbled out into the hallway, her heart pounding, her feet going quickly, blindly down the stairs. *It can't be him — it can't be —* yet he'd been playing with her up there, *toying* with her, and all the fears caved in on her and she nearly fell because she didn't see the last step.

She grabbed for the bannister and kept going, sure now that she'd never come back to this house again. *But that will look suspicious . . . if you just run out of here, you'll look more suspicious than ever and everyone will wonder why and what will you tell them —*

"I don't know," Belinda whispered to herself. "Oh, I don't know . . . I don't know."

She jerked open the front door and yelled back over her shoulder, "Mr. Cobbs, I'm leaving now!"

And she was still looking back over her shoulder when she ran full force into something on the porch, when a pair of arms went around her to keep her from falling.

"Hey," a voice laughed, "where's the fire?"

And Belinda stared up into soft hazel eyes, sun-bleached hair . . . and a teasing smile only inches away from her open mouth.

Chapter 7

"One thing I like about coming home" — the boy looked amused — "I never know what surprises I'll find."

Behind her Belinda heard the perfectly measured steps of Cobbs approaching. She looked back and saw him there in the entryway, a suitcase in each hand.

"Hi, Cobbs," the boy grinned.

"Mister Noel," Cobbs nodded, as if it were the most normal thing in the world. "Allowance running low again?"

"Now what kind of a welcome is that?" Noel chided good-naturedly. "I like *this* one a *lot* better." He let go of Belinda's shoulders, and she blushed as he stepped past her into the hall. "So what's all this? Did you finally throw Mom out?"

"Your mother's just leaving, sir. On business."

"Great. This'd be a perfect time for you to make your escape —"

"Noel!" The voice came from above and was so startled that they all looked up to the balcony. Mrs. Thorne's face seemed to be making its usual struggle between civility and annoyance, but she came quickly down the stairs, her arms regally wide. "Darling — what a surprise!"

"Hi, Mom." Noel looked extremely embarrassed, and Cobbs tactfully redirected his gaze toward the ceiling.

"Why are you here? What do you need? You should have told me you were coming." Her eyes raked him from head to foot, her mouth set in a tight smile. "If you came for Fred's sake, there's nothing you can do."

"I finished up early at school." He shrugged. "And how *is* Fred? Any change?"

"I'm afraid not. And you've wasted a perfectly good visit, too. I'm just now leaving." Mrs. Thorne sighed. "New York, of all places. How long will you be here?"

"I don't really know, Mom. I have a little time before my job starts so — "

"Oh, job!" she said scornfully. "As if you needed to work."

"I like to work," he said firmly. He went over to Cobbs and offered his hand. "How've you been, Cobbs?"

"Peachy."

Noel grinned again and turned back to his mother. "So who's this frantic young lady, and why's she running away?"

They all looked at her, and Belinda went even redder. Mrs. Thorne gave an exasperated shrug, her bracelets rattling in the direction of the upstairs hall.

"Oh, it's probably Adam —"

"Adam?" Noel looked surprised. "Is Adam here?"

"Oh, really, it's most tragic!" Mrs. Thorne jerked on her coat and gloves, tilted a hat onto her head. "He's *staying* here, of all things. I don't know for how long, either, but his mother sent him because of Fred and —"

"She means the accident," Belinda spoke up, trying to control the anger in her voice. "She means the *accident* was the most tragic thing." As Mrs. Thorne looked taken aback, Cobbs flicked a look at Belinda and then onto his shoes.

Mrs. Thorne headed for the door. "Fred . . . this damn business . . . now Adam. . . . It's always something, Noel — do I have an easy life?"

Noel hid a smile and trailed behind her, stopping again as his mother let out a shriek. Belinda stepped out onto the porch just in time to see a brown blur leap from the red sportscar in the driveway.

"What *is* that — you *didn't* — oh, Noel, how *could* you —"

"Relax, Mom, you won't even be here to notice her," Noel chuckled. There was a loud bark, and a moment later a huge dog bounded past her into the house. Belinda recognized it as the dog in Noel's photograph, and as Noel let out a sharp whistle, the dog loped out again and leaped back into his car. Cobbs sighed and started to put the luggage into the Mercedes, but Noel stopped him.

"I can take her, Cobbs. Just put the stuff in my car."

"If you're sure it's convenient, sir."

"I'm positive. Take the afternoon off or something."

Cobbs hesitated. "Actually . . . I would like to stop by the hospital and inquire after Mr. Thorne — "

"Go ahead. Stay as long as you want. I'll get her where she needs to go on time."

Mrs. Thorne brightened. "Oh, darling, how very sweet of you — it'll give us a chance to talk and catch up. I miss you when I don't see you, you know that." She blew him an absentminded little kiss as Cobbs reached to open the other door.

Noel's smile seemed oddly forced. "Sure you do, Mom," he said, more to himself than to her. He turned to Belinda with an apologetic shrug. "Sorry about all this chaos. I'm Noel Ashby. And you're —"

"She's Belinda Swanson," Mrs. Thorne said. "Do hurry, and let's get going —"

"Nice to meet you, Belinda." This time the smile was genuine, the grip strong yet gentle as he shook her hand. "I guess I missed something — *was* there a reason you were running out of the house?"

Belinda fumbled for an answer, conscious of Mrs. Thorne's disapproving look. "I . . . I had something to do — I forgot — I had to get home."

"Oh, then, I've probably made you late. I'm sorry."

"No, that's all right, you didn't." She smiled at his concern.

"Where's your car? Did you drive over?"

"Noel —" his mother said impatiently.

"No, I took the bus," Belinda said.

"I'll take her home, sir." Cobbs started back toward the other car.

"No, I'll take her. It's the least I can do."

"Honestly, Noel!" Mrs. Thorne fumed. "*Who* is going to take *me* —"

"Just hang on, Mom. Go inside and make yourself comfortable — I'll be right back."

"But the plane —"

"I'm sure we have plenty of time, don't we, Cobbs?"

"Oodles."

"Oh, no, you don't have to do that," Belinda protested. "It's not far, really . . . I'll just —"

"I don't trust buses," Noel said firmly, digging in his jeans pockets for his keys. "They're not safe, and you can never count on the schedules. Come on. This place always gives me a craving for fresh air." He gave her a conspiratorial wink as his mother went back into the house.

Belinda hesitated, then gave in to a laugh. "Okay, then. Thanks."

"Oh, and this is Sasha. Sasha — Belinda. Hope you like dogs."

"I love dogs."

"Then Sasha and I are your friends for life, right, Sash?"

Sasha gave a happy bark as they climbed into the car, and Noel brushed frantically at the dog hair on the front seat.

"So I make allowances," he grinned. "She's my best girl."

Belinda smiled back and settled herself comfortably beside him, but as she looked back at the house she saw something move at one of the upstairs windows. A curtain pulling back . . . a silhouette watching them leave. She shivered and glanced over at Noel. Apparently he hadn't noticed it; he was too busy fooling with the tape deck.

"I haven't been here in a while." Noel tried to peer around Sasha, who had managed to squeeze herself between the bucket seats. "I always go through the park first before anything else. It's one of my favorite places."

"So . . . you've lived here a long time."

He shook his head. "No, we lived in Washington before Mom married Fred. But I've been here for holidays and things. I really like the town, but I'm usually not here long enough to look it all over. How about you?"

"I was born here. My mom's a nurse at Charity Hospital."

"I see. Now, maybe it's none of my business, but I'm still a little confused. How do you know Adam?"

"Well," Belinda looked away, "we're not really friends."

Noel's glance was surprised. "No? Oh, sorry, I just assumed —"

"I'm just helping him study. Mrs. Thorne hired me to be his tutor, since he can't go to school."

"That should be fun," Noel said offhandedly, then glanced at her. "Oh. Sorry again."

"So you don't like him, either?"

"Hey . . . I didn't say that. He's . . . different."

"He won't let me see him. He keeps his room dark, and he won't let anyone close to him. I think Cobbs brings him pain medicine." On a sudden hunch she asked, "Do you know Adam very well?"

Noel's head went slowly from side to side. "I guess it sounds kind of funny, but we haven't really been around each other that much. Mom married Fred — my stepdad — just three years ago. I've been away at school — and I think Adam's been living with his mother ever since his folks split up years ago."

"Do you . . . do you happen to know where his mother lives?"

"No, I've never been there. I don't think it's far, though. Some little town."

"But where? Close to here?"

Noel gave her a strange look. "Why? Are you planning a visit or something?"

"No," she said, flustered. "I'm just curious."

His eyes flicked back to the road. "I don't know. A couple hours' drive, maybe. I really don't know."

Belinda flinched, her voice coming out taut. "I don't think he likes it here very much."

"Well" — Noel looked almost sympathetic — "I can't really blame him. My mom's pretty hard to take most of the time." He adjusted the volume control, his fingers tapping a rhythm on the steering wheel. "So how long is he staying, do *you* know?"

She shook her head. "He's . . . he's really a very scary person sometimes. . . ."

"Ah. From what I've heard, the wreck didn't have anything to do with *that*." Noel threw her another quick glance. "From what I've heard, Adam's never been known for his charming personality."

Belinda pondered this, remembering the photograph in the kitchen. "From what you've *heard* or from what you *know?*"

Noel smiled. "Our only thing in common is having a parent and a stepparent. The times we *have* been in the same house, we never spend time together. Adam's a real loner. I don't think he has any use for people."

"Haven't you ever just talked?"

"No. Like I said, all I really know about Adam is what I've heard." He hesitated and glanced at her. "Look, I don't want to give you any unfair impressions of Adam. He's not here to defend himself, and I don't know him, it's that simple."

"I have my own impressions." Belinda sighed. "I want to help him, but he doesn't want me to. I don't know if I should come back or not."

Noel shifted his shoulders. "And I'm not being much help at all, am I? I don't know what to *tell* you."

"Oh, this is my street." Belinda straightened, pointing. "Last house — the green shutters." She tried not to feel embarrassed by him being here — after the kind of house he was used to, she was sure this neighborhood looked near poverty level to him. Asking Noel in was out of the question.

"Belinda?"

She was already out of the car. He leaned across Sasha as Belinda looked back in the window, and his hand reached up to touch her arm.

"I know this is none of my business," he began hesitantly, "but this thing with Adam — he's been through a bad time, and I don't imagine he's over it yet. If I can do anything . . . you know . . . I hope you'll tell me."

Belinda tried to smile. "Maybe," she said lamely. "Thanks for the offer."

"You think about it." He started to back up, then stopped again. "And if you *do* decide to come, why don't I pick you up?"

"That's nice of you, but there's a bus that runs right past my school."

"It wouldn't be any trouble — "

"Thanks. Really. But I can take the bus all right."

He waved and honked the horn, a blur of shiny red fading down the street. Belinda stood there looking after him, then let herself in with a sigh. *Yes, I could definitely get serious about Noel. . . . "Noel and Belinda"* — it sounded good, she decided, and then *who are you kidding, Belinda Swanson; you're as ordinary as they come.*

Laughing at herself, she went out to get the mail, her shoulders hunched against the chilly twilight. She took a deep breath of air and waved at a passing neighbor, plunging her other hand into the mailbox.

Something oozed beneath her fingers.

As Belinda gasped and jerked away, she looked wildly back at the sidewalk but the neighbor had gone; the street was empty.

And then she looked down at her hand.

There were wet globs of red on her fingers . . .

and the smell made her gag and step back off the curb.

Belinda stared at the mailbox in horror.

It's Frank playing a joke again . . . it has to be Frank . . . some sick, stupid joke and damn you, Frank, for what you got us into —

She couldn't put her hand back in there. Yet — whatever it was — she couldn't leave it inside.

Carefully she listened, but nothing moved. The thing in the mailbox was dead — it had to be dead — and by the smell of it, had been dead a long time.

Slowly she eased her fingers inside . . . groping . . . groping . . . she felt something soft beneath the slime.

Holding her breath, she cupped her palm around it and lifted it out.

The scream she'd been holding back rose into her throat and stuck there, the awful, hideous thing in her hand looking back at her beneath a smeared coating of mashed entrails.

It was a head.

Once it had been part of a doll.

Once it had probably been beautiful.

Only now its face had been slashed repeatedly and someone had stitched it sloppily back together with thick, black thread.

It was grinning at her.

And where its eyes should have been, there were only deep, black holes.

Chapter 8

"Okay, Hildy, start talking."

Belinda's voice was surprisingly calm as she turned the plastic bag upside down beside Hildy. The doll's head fell out with a thud, and Hildy gagged, scooting back on the bench.

"Belinda, are you *crazy*? Get that thing *away* from me!"

"I mean it, Hildy, I want to know the truth." Belinda squatted on the grass in front of her and ignored the first bell as the campus cleared. Hildy's mouth dropped open in surprise.

"This isn't a joke?"

"You tell me. Someone put it in my mailbox yesterday." She shuddered at the memory, but kept her eyes on the other girl's face. "Hildy?"

"Oh, God, Belinda — it's making me sick —" Hildy got down on the ground beside her and clutched at her stomach. "Look, there's Frank now. Why don't you ask *him*?"

"Truants! Get to class!" Frank flashed his most disarming grin, and bent to give Hildy a kiss. "My fan club awaits me and —" As his senses suddenly became aware of the doll's head, his whole face looked repulsed. "What the hell is *that?*"

"I was hoping you could tell me," Belinda said coolly.

Frank stared at her for a long moment, a faint touch of mockery flickering in his eyes. "Oh, so I see I'm still on your hit list, huh, Belinda?"

"Come on, Frank, if you did it, just say so."

"Well, aren't we feeling just a tiny bit paranoid today?" He kicked out at the head, sending it rolling onto the ground. Its sockets gaped up at him. "Is this supposed to remind me of something?"

"Frank, please." Hildy grabbed his arm. "We'd all like to just forget —"

"Yeah? Well, tell that to your neurotic friend here. Tell *her* to forget it instead of driving the rest of us nuts."

"Frank!" Hildy pleaded, but he shook her off, throwing one arm around Belinda and pulling her close.

"If *anyone* finds out *anything,*" he smiled sweetly, leaning down into Belinda's face, "it'll be because of *you*. And you wouldn't want anything to happen to *me*, would you, Belinda? Because *you* know and *I* know, that *you* still think I'm pretty wonderful —"

"Oh, Frank, just stop it." Belinda pushed at him, but he held her tighter, his grin widening.

"You think about what's at stake here — if any questions come up, *I* wasn't the one driving, *remember?*"

The look on Hildy's face was positively stricken. Belinda saw it through a haze of anger, and thought for a split second that Hildy was going to faint.

"And I *promise* you, Belinda Swanson," Frank added, his finger wagging back and forth, playfully, in front of her face, "I'll swear *Hildy* wasn't driving, either."

Belinda felt numb as he sauntered away. She was trembling all over, drenched in cold sweat. Hildy was as pale as marble, and as Belinda prodded the doll's head back into the bag with her shoe, Hildy reached weakly for her arm.

"Belinda . . . just don't pay any attention to him, okay? He's just being —"

"Frank," Belinda sounded more drained than angry. "When are you going to stop making excuses for him?"

"He had a bad day at practice yesterday," Hildy went on as if she hadn't heard. "He's always weird when he's been bad at practice."

"Oh, Hildy . . ." On an impulse Belinda leaned over and hugged her friend tightly. "Why don't you come over later. I haven't even had a chance to tell you about Noel."

It worked, as she knew it would. Hildy perked up.

"Who's Noel?"

"Mrs. Thorne's son. He came home yesterday. He has this wonderful dog named Sasha and —"

"Forget the dog — I want to hear all about this guy." She laughed, her old self again. "How about seven?"

"Perfect. I'll get pizza."

"And I won't bring Frank."

They laughed and ran to class, but Belinda found it hard to concentrate on anything. She'd dumped the doll's head in the trash, but the memory wouldn't go away that easily. Every time she tried to keep her mind on her books, the image of Adam would snake into her thoughts, and she debated whether to even go back to his house today.

But I have to find out the truth . . . and I have to help Adam. . . . If Belinda thought it once, she thought it a hundred times — and she was still thinking it when she got off at her bus stop that afternoon. *I'll wait you out, Adam Thorne, I'll wait you out even if it kills me.*

But Cobbs didn't look particularly encouraging when he met her at the door.

"You *are* a glutton for punishment," he said dryly.

"How is he today?"

"At his most enchanting: unconscious."

"Oh . . . the medicine. Darn it, Cobbs, what am I going to do?" Belinda sighed and plopped down on the porch, spilling her books at Cobbs's feet. She waited for him to answer, but when he didn't, she glanced up into his thin, old face.

What she saw there made her draw back . . . and stare.

For just a fleeting instant — no more — he'd had the strangest, almost frightening look in his eyes.

"Cobbs?" she murmured.

"Perhaps you should leave, miss."

"What?"

"And never come back here."

Belinda's laugh was strained. "That sounds like some kind of warning or something."

"Does it?" Cobbs drew himself up even straighter. And then the mask was back again, settling stiffly over the sharp features of his face. "I need to shut the door," he said.

"Does that mean you're going to throw me out?"

"It means you might as well come inside."

Watching him now, it was as if their brief exchange had never taken place. Belinda nodded and followed him into the kitchen. Sasha was peeking in one of the patio doors, barking a welcome, and Belinda wondered where Noel was.

"Please, Cobbs, could I let her in? She looks so lonely out there."

"It would thrill me no end."

Smiling to herself, Belinda opened the door, and was immediately bowled over by the delighted dog. For several minutes she sat there on the kitchen floor scratching Sasha's ears while Cobbs stacked plates in the cabinets.

"Tea, miss?"

"I'd love some. But only if you have some, too."

"As you wish."

"Have you heard from Mrs. Thorne? Will she be in New York a long time?"

"One can only hope." Cobbs put the kettle on to boil and began unloading the dishwasher.

"This is probably awful of me, but I'm glad she's

gone," Belinda thought out loud. "I'll bet she's hard to work for."

"Attila the Hun would be a dream."

Belinda looked back at him and laughed. "If you don't like her, why do you even stay?"

"I work for Mr. Thorne, miss. And as long as he is my employer, I stay."

Belinda read the unspoken message. "I'm sorry, Cobbs. Is there any change?" She put her nose against Sasha's fur as he shook his head.

"It's difficult when one can do nothing." He rinsed out a dishrag and slowly began wiping the counter-top as Belinda scooted closer to him across the floor. Sasha climbed into her lap, spilling comfortably over each knee.

"I don't like feeling helpless," Belinda murmured. "It's one of the worst feelings in the world. If I can ever . . . well . . . you know . . . if you ever need to talk. . . ."

"I'll alert you straightaway."

Belinda smiled at the sarcasm and hugged Sasha's soft neck. "But it's nice to have someone to talk to. Like you and me talking now —" She glanced away, embarrassed. "My best friend and I don't talk anymore. My mom's never home. Did you and Mr. Thorne talk a lot?"

Cobbs shook his head, poured the tea. "The Thornes have always been uncomfortable with de-monstrativeness. I was needed, and I did my best for him."

"I'll bet you mean a lot to him. Even though he

never showed it." Belinda looked wistful. "You'd mean a lot to me."

This time Cobbs stopped. He stood rigidly at the table as if her remark had caught him offguard. After a moment he said, "Mr. Thorne was a selfish man. A driven man. Still, in his own way . . . I like to think he cared."

Belinda nodded. She felt sad. "So what will you do? Work for Mrs. Thorne?"

"God forbid."

He pulled out a chair and waited for her to sit. Sasha got up obligingly and resettled herself under the table at Belinda's feet. For a while there was only the clink of china cups and the gentle silence of sharing.

"I worry about Adam," Belinda said at last. "I worry that he's so full of hate."

"It has nothing to do with you."

But it might, Cobbs, if might have everything to do with me. She met his eyes unhappily. "I don't know what to do — I can't force him to see me. But he really needs a friend, don't you think?"

"He wouldn't know a friend if he stepped on one . . . which I'm certain he's done many times."

"But . . . shouldn't I try?"

"Drink your tea."

Puzzled, Belinda drained her cup. She closed her eyes, savoring the last mouthful, then opened them again to see Cobbs watching her.

"I like you, Cobbs," Belinda said quietly. "You're really nice. You're . . . you know . . . easy to talk to."

"One of my many talents, miss." He reached for the teapot but Belinda shook her head.

"No thanks, I should get home. If Adam won't study, there's no reason for me to hang around, I guess."

"Gracious, no," Cobbs rolled his eyes. "Especially now that you've taken your afternoon refreshment."

She couldn't be sure, but she almost thought she'd seen a twinkle far back in his eye. She gathered her things, giving Sasha a last fond pat.

"I hope you don't think I'm taking you for granted, Cobbs. You happen to be the high point of my day."

"Naturally. Now if you'll allow me to drive you —"

"Thanks, but I'll catch the bus." She glanced toward the stairs on their way out. "I guess I'll try again tomorrow — maybe he'll be in a better mood —"

"I'll hold my breath." Cobbs opened the door for her, peering out into the late afternoon. "It's getting very gloomy —"

"Oh, don't worry. I always take a shortcut through the park — it saves a lot of time —"

"A shortcut?" he frowned. "A safe one, I assume."

"Oh, sure, I don't think too many people know about it — it's an old parking lot on the east side of the park. Well, see you tomorrow!" She started down the drive, but almost at once had that feeling of being watched. At the street she pretended to check her books just so she could glance at that upstairs window without being obvious.

Nothing moved.

No shadow withdrew into the darkness beyond.

Unsettled, Belinda started off again, her mind buzzing with frustrations. What was she going to do about Adam? How would she ever get close to him if he wouldn't let her? And why had Cobbs said what he did, about her never going back to that house? He'd looked so different when he'd said it . . . almost *sinister*, she realized now.

Belinda forced the thoughts away as she hurried through the park. She hadn't realized how really dark it was — she hadn't meant to stay so long talking with Cobbs. The park seemed more deserted than usual this evening . . . the only sounds were of distant traffic and birds settling themselves for the night. Belinda glanced up and felt a twinge of uneasiness. Low clouds were gathering, swept along by a chilly breeze, playing hide-and-seek with a pale sprinkling of early stars. She let herself through the secret opening in the fence, hoping she could make it to the bus stop while there was still enough light to see by.

Her shoes made staccato sounds on the pavement — sharp clicks that stabbed at her raw nerves. She hated the echo of footsteps when there were no others to join them. They made her so terribly aware of her aloneness. . . .

She walked faster, her heart pounding.

Silly . . . you've been this way lots of times. . . .

Except tonight it seemed different for some reason. Tonight she had a strange feeling of dread that she'd never had before.

Forcing back a shiver, she kept her eyes straight ahead, on the fence at the opposite end of the lot. All around her, sad heaps of junk crouched like sluggish animals, their hulking shapes ominous against the fast-darkening sky. As Belinda focused in on her destination, she could hear the whine of wind through rusted pipes, the occasional scurrying of some startled animal . . .

The soft, steady hum of a motor.

She stopped, suddenly alert, every nerve prickling. For just one wild moment she was sure she'd heard the sound of a car . . . an engine purring beneath the hushed sounds of evening.

She looked around, eyes straining through the dusk, probing the shapeless blobs of shadow that hemmed her in.

Nothing moved. The lot was as still as a cemetery.

Swallowing fear, Belinda began to run. All logic told her she was being ridiculous, that she couldn't really have heard the sound of a car — but as she glanced back over her shoulder, a scream rose up in her throat.

One long, low shadow was oozing out from the others . . . and gliding after her across the concrete. . . .

"Oh, God —" As panic exploded inside her, Belinda flung herself forward, every instinct targeted on the fence twenty yards ahead. She could hear her footsteps pounding in her ears, her breath ragged in her throat — as she took another look behind her, a new burst of fear shook her from head to toe.

It really was a car.

Only, now, curiously, frighteningly, it didn't seem to be coming after her — only sitting there in the gloom . . . patiently . . . waiting.

Without warning Belinda tripped, sprawling onto the pavement, purse and books flying in all directions. As she got painfully to her knees and grabbed at her things, a sudden glare of light blinded her and pinned her to the ground.

The car's headlights were on.

Like huge spotlights they trapped her there as she threw up her hands to shield her eyes.

Helplessly, Belinda twisted herself out of their way, scraping her arms and face as she lay flat, mind racing, wondering what to do. At any minute she expected to hear the engine start up, to see the phantom car bearing down on her —

But instead there was only deep, endless silence . . . and that was most terrifying of all.

"Who are you?" Belinda screamed. "What do you want?"

Beyond the circles of light, the night stilled and deepened. Choking back a sob, Belinda pressed her face against folded arms, gathering all her strength to jump up and escape.

And then the lights went out.

As suddenly as the darkness had been shattered,

it closed in around her once more . . . thick . . . secretive . . . safe.

She only hesitated a moment, to test the air, to listen for footsteps, or an engine approaching through cover of night —

And then, dazed, Belinda began to run.

Chapter 9

"Cobbs!"

Belinda staggered up to the front door and fell against the bell. The handle was locked. There were lights on inside but she couldn't hear anyone, and Sasha wasn't barking.

"Cobbs, please let me in!"

She stepped back dizzily and nearly fell off the porch.

The back. Maybe the patio door isn't locked.

It took a while to follow the sprawling layout of the house, and when she finally came up against a wall of shrubbery, it took another ten minutes to find a way to get through. She didn't even know why she'd come back to the house — all she knew was that she couldn't wait alone on a dark corner for the bus, and at least Cobbs was here —

"Cobbs! Please let me in! It's Belinda!"

She saw the opening then.

With a sob of relief, she fell onto the patio — saw the tall, stiff figure framed in the kitchen doorway —

"Oh, Cobbs," she cried, "something terrible happened —"

But it wasn't Cobbs who pulled himself from the shadows, his features caught in the light from the room behind him.

It was Adam.

And now Belinda looked clearly into his face.

It was a cruel face — and even without the mutilations, she sensed that it would still be a cruel face, for the cruelty looked back at her from deep, deep in his eyes. She saw the stitches lacing his sunken cheeks, his forehead, and his chin — the purple-yellow bruises around his black, fathomless eyes — the lines of pain etched jaggedly and permanently into his rugged features. He was the Adam in the photograph . . . and yet he was chillingly different.

"You don't give up, do you?" Adam sounded amused and — Belinda realized uneasily — not particularly surprised to see her. "Well, take a good look. Remember it in your dreams."

Something moved near his neck, and as Belinda's eyes were drawn to the subtle motion, she was horrified to see a snake hanging there.

"Someone . . ." With an effort, she looked away. "I think someone was following me. . . ." And now her eyes moved slowly over his legs, his feet, over his cane, and his strong, gentle hands gripping it. Even in his condition, there was something so sensual about him that it was almost magnetic.

"Following you?" Adam's eyes widened slightly. His mouth curled at the corners. "You should be more careful going out at night. All alone. Anything could happen."

Belinda forced her gaze out onto the patio. "Where's Cobbs?"

"At the store. But please come in. Maybe I can help."

"No." Her voice quivered, though she fought to control it. "No. Just call a cab for me, please."

There was a moment's hesitation as his eyes flicked over her.

"You're bleeding. Come inside." Adam limped slowly into the kitchen, but Belinda stayed where she was.

"Just please call a cab."

"We'd better take care of your face first. You wouldn't want to end up looking like me, now, would you?" He disappeared from her view, returning a minute later with a bottle of alcohol and some cotton. Belinda swallowed, forcing down her fear. The snake's trail brushed over the table.

I'll go in and make the call myself . . . I'll leave the door open . . .

"This person following you," Adam said slowly, unscrewing the cap on the bottle, "what did he look like?"

"I didn't see him."

"Oh . . . pity. Then there wasn't anything about him you recognized."

"He was in a car," Belinda said shakily. "He started after me, but then he stopped. He put the headlights on."

Adam balanced himself against the table . . . tipped the bottle onto some cotton.

"How lucky you got away."

"When he turned the headlights off, I ran — I got back into the park and came here —" She broke off suddenly, her attention caught by something shiny lying on a counter near a back door.

A set of keys.

"Where does that door go to?" she asked quietly.

Adam's glance was disinterested. "The garage. Don't worry, Belinda, you can run in any direction and get away from me quite easily." He pushed back a chair, made a mock bow. "Sit down."

"I'd rather stand."

His eyes fastened on her face, and with an effort she held his gaze. It seemed forever that he watched her. At last she gave in to his stare and sat, a chill working up her spine as the snake crawled slowly over his chest.

"Such a mess," Adam scolded gently. "You should stay away from shortcuts."

Belinda glanced at him sharply, searching his face, finding nothing. He ran one cotton swab slowly down her cheek. She felt fire and ice and her hands gripped the edge of the table.

"How do you know that?" she asked weakly. "How do you know about the shortcut?"

"Cobbs told me." There was a sharp sting as he held the cotton against her skin. "You should be more careful, Belinda. You could get hurt."

She bit her lip, trying not to look at him. His

expert fingers worked slowly up each side of her face . . . methodical . . . deliberate. His touch was light — almost teasing — yet underneath she felt cold steel, a frightening strength barely held in check.

"Please don't do any more. My mom can take care of it —"

"Your mom's not home. She's working double shifts at the hospital, and she doesn't get off till seven A.M. The rest of the time . . . you're all alone in the house."

Belinda's heart jumped, her grip tightening on the table edge. *Did I tell him that? Did Cobbs? How does he know?*

"I know a lot about you, Belinda." Adam's fingers lingered against her cheek. His other hand slid slowly down her neck, sending shivers through her, until it finally clamped down upon her shoulder. "And isn't it strange . . . but I keep feeling I've seen you somewhere before?"

She couldn't move.

Suddenly she was so terrified that all she could hear was her own frantically beating pulse. A scream struggled into her throat — her voice came out over it, shrill and broken.

"I . . . I don't see how you could —"

"You sound nervous, Belinda." To her horror he leaned down, slowly, into her face. She could feel his calm, even breath . . . the chill from his eyes. "And I'm trying to figure out," he whispered, "just what it is about me that makes you feel that way?"

Around his neck the snake roused . . . body pulling into itself . . . head slowly lifting. Its forked tongue darted inches from her face.

"Yes . . ." Adam murmured, "you'd be surprised at the things I know."

"You're hurting me," she whispered.

"Am I?" The black eyes lifted. "Oh. Sorry."

"What's going on in here?" The voice came unexpectedly from the doorway, and as Noel stood there surveying the scene, an angry frown crossed his face. "Belinda — are you all right? What happened?"

"Oh, Noel —" It was all she could do to keep from throwing herself into his arms. As she stumbled from the table she saw his eyes settle furiously on Adam.

"What the hell do you think you're doing? Get that thing away from her."

"Belinda's shaking," Adam said, half smiling. "I think I scared her."

"What happened?" Noel demanded again. He didn't look at all in the mood for Adam's games, and as Belinda got to him, he caught her by the shoulders, reviewing her disheveled appearance with dismay. "Look at your face — what — ?"

She shook her head. "I'm okay, really. Someone scared me in the park and —"

"She took a shortcut." Adam slid a caress over the snake's supple body. "She should know better. There're all kinds of weird people out there."

"Come on." Noel put his arm around her, flashing Adam a cold stare. "I'll take you home."

"But we haven't had a chance to talk yet, " Adam

said with mock pleading. "She's always asking me about my accident — now that she's seen this amazing face, she should know how it happened."

"Come on," Noel said again, but once more Adam's voice stopped them.

"You probably wouldn't know the place, Belinda — it's not even around here. In fact, it's a two-hour drive away."

"Please," Belinda tugged on Noel's sleeve. "Let's go now."

"What's the matter?" Adam smiled. "Is the suspense too much for you?"

Noel's eyes sparked dangerously. "Cut it out, Adam. I don't know what you're trying to prove, but —"

"I don't have to prove anything. Here's proof." Adam pointed to his face . . . to his legs. "And here —"

"Take me home," Belinda mumbled.

"What's the matter, Belinda? I thought you wanted to hear all the gory details —"

"Please, Adam, I don't want to know —"

"How my father screamed? I haven't told you yet about my father screaming —"

"Stop it —"

"I was just picking them up at the airport. Dad and dear old Gloria. I live around there, you know. They wanted to see me, so I offered to drive them home. . . . It was raining, I think . . ."

"Adam, *stop* it!"

"Ever been sliced through your face? Ever had your legs crushed — ?"

"Don't, Adam, *please!* I'm sorry! I'm *sorry!*" Belinda began to cry, and Noel shoved her through the door, throwing a murderous look over his shoulder.

"Jesus, Adam, how do you live with yourself —"

"I cover the mirrors." A slow, chilling smile crawled over his face. The snake slid over his shoulder . . . down his arm. "And by the way," he murmured, shaking his head slowly . . . slowly . . . "Why do you think Belinda looks so familiar to me? Do you think I could have seen her somewhere before?"

Chapter 10

"God, Belinda, I'm sorry. I don't know what gets into him."

Belinda, huddled in her corner of the front seat, shook her head miserably. "It's okay." *Oh, Noel, I need to tell you, but I can't — what am I going to do?* "I just want to go home."

"Back up a minute. I want to know what happened tonight in the park."

"Someone was chasing me. Someone in a car — well, not chasing me, exactly — I mean, they sat there with the headlights on and —" She glanced at him, determined not to start crying. "I'm not making any sense at all. Never mind. Nothing happened and I'm all right and —"

"I don't call that 'all right.' " Noel put one hand carefully to her face. "Shouldn't you go to a doctor or something?"

"It's just a scrape — I fell down in the parking lot, that's all." She rubbed the raw places on her palms and blurted out, "Does Adam ever get out of the house?"

Noel looked at her in surprise. "Only when Cobbs takes him."

"But what about this evening? Was he out this evening?"

"Cobbs was," Noel sounded puzzled. "Adam's been home all day. Why?"

"Oh . . . no reason . . . I . . ." She pressed her mouth into a thin line. "No reason, it's — what's so funny?"

Noel, struggling to hide a smile, had the grace to look sheepish. "Sorry . . . it just sounded so funny — like maybe Adam escapes when no one's watching."

Even Belinda had to laugh at that, but Noel's next comment stopped her cold.

"Why'd you ask that, anyway? You almost sound as if you suspect him of something."

"Well, of course I don't. Why should I?" She wished Noel would stop asking questions; she was getting all confused. Even now she could see Adam's face . . . the shrewd look in his eyes as he'd thrown things out at her so easily. It wasn't the first time he'd toyed with her. It was something he was good at.

It was something he enjoyed.

"Hey, you okay?"

She jumped as Noel's hand closed over her own, then gave him an embarrassed smile.

"Just a little nervous."

"After what happened, I can understand why. Look, Belinda, if Adam makes you that upset . . . if you don't want to come back to the house anymore

. . . well, personally I think Adam just gets a kick out of scaring people —"

She nodded tiredly. "So I shouldn't give him the satisfaction."

"He probably wouldn't pick on you so much if he thought it didn't bother you."

"You're right — I don't want him to think he's intimidating me — and besides, I promised your mother —"

"Forget that. She hates Adam anyway; it won't matter to her." He changed lanes and checked the rearview mirror. "And speaking of Mom, I'm kind of surprised I haven't heard from her. New York must have been more interesting than she thought."

Belinda nodded without hearing.

It can't be the same wreck . . . it's just too much of a coincidence, and no matter what Adam says, I won't believe it —

"Belinda?" Noel glanced at her, half laughing. "Did you fall asleep on me just then?"

"Oh, sorry." Belinda tried to smile. "My mind just wandered off for a minute."

"You need to get some rest," Noel said gently. "Being with Adam very long can't be good for your health."

"The gate," Belinda said suddenly, and again Noel cast her a wary look. "The gate to your house — when I ran back, it was open." *Open. Like he was waiting for me.*

Noel shook his head. "It couldn't have been. That gate's never open."

"But it was tonight. I walked right in."

Noel looked puzzled. "Maybe Cobbs left it open accidentally when he left. It's not very likely . . . but it is possible, I guess. Poor old guy's pretty upset about Fred."

Belinda wasn't convinced. "Yes . . . I guess so. . . ."

"So what about the gate?" Noel turned into her driveway and let the motor idle. "There must be some perfectly logical reason why all of a sudden you're so worried about our gate." The look he gave her was amused, and Belinda blushed.

"I just wouldn't want anyone wandering in, that's all," she said lamely. "It's not safe . . . and Adam's there alone sometimes — and —"

"Ah. So now we're *concerned* about Adam."

Belinda couldn't tell if Noel was teasing or a trifle put out. Quickly she added, "Well, he can't run, can he? If someone broke in and went after him?"

"No, he can't run. He can't even get around without that cane. Going up and down those stairs is pure torture for him."

"Well, then, see? You should just make sure the gate's locked so Adam doesn't get hurt."

"Right." Noel cast her a strange look. "By all means, my first priority will be for Adam's safety."

"And for yours, of course. I meant yours, too."

"Oh, thanks very much. I'm touched." This time Noel grinned, briefly covering her hand with his own. Relieved, Belinda saw Hildy's car pull up, and she got out.

"Thanks, Noel. I really mean it."

"Well . . . sure . . . can I call you?"

"Yes. I'd like that." Hoping she wouldn't seem rude, Belinda hurried to Hildy's car as her friend got out, and then she waved as Noel drove away.

"Who was that?" Hildy wanted to know.

"Noel."

"And I missed him! You traitor. Gosh, you look awful." Hildy peered at her closely as they went into the house. "Did some cat get to your face?"

"Someone came after me in the park tonight. In a car."

"Oh, no, Belinda." Hildy's eyes locked on hers, lips moving but nothing more coming out.

"I'm not kidding. I ran all the way back to the Thornes.' Someone knew I'd be taking the shortcut tonight — they *had* to know, and —"

"Wait a minute. Who would know that? Whoever you saw could have been the police. Or a mugger. Anyone could have been hiding in the parking lot —"

"Adam knew."

"But I thought Adam couldn't walk." Hildy looked confused.

"He can't." For a long while they stared at each other, then, little by little, Belinda told Hildy all that had happened. When she finally finished, Hildy sank back on the couch.

"I can't believe it," she sighed. "It just doesn't make sense. Those things that Adam said to you — it *sounds* like it was the same accident, but . . ."

"And those keys were there. The gate was open."

"And Cobbs was gone, you said."

"But Noel said Adam had been there all evening."

"God, it's just too weird. It's almost like someone *else* knows — and they're trying to scare you."

Belinda's look was accusing. "Are you thinking what I'm thinking?"

Hildy mouthed the word reluctantly. "Frank?"

"Or whoever was watching on the hill that night."

For a moment they were silent. Belinda closed her eyes, completely drained.

"I forgot the pizza."

"Forget about the pizza. I'll call and have one delivered. This is totally bizarre, you know. You shouldn't have even gone back to their house."

"I was afraid to wait for a bus. I was scared to be by myself."

"You should have called me."

"Oh, right." Belinda's glance was scathing. "You've been so supportive till now, believing everything I say."

Hildy sat there with her head down. Belinda bit her lip and looked away. After several minutes Hildy got up and went into the kitchen, and Belinda heard her dialing the telephone.

"Oh, God, what's happening?" Belinda whispered to herself. "What am I going to do?' She reached up and cautiously touched her face, the scratches tender and swollen. She remembered Adam's fingers there, and a shiver went through her. Even thinking about it now made her feel weak and terrified.

"Everyone must be ordering pizza tonight," Hildy stood in the doorway, as if she couldn't quite make up her mind to come in. "It'll be about forty-five minutes."

"That's okay. I'm not very hungry."

"Maybe you will be by then." Hildy walked slowly to the couch, staring down at Belinda's bowed head. "Do you think it was the same accident?"

"Yes. I do."

"And do you . . ." Hildy looked surprisingly near tears now — "do you think Adam knows it was us that night?"

"I think he knows it was me."

"But — but —"

"Adam thinks he's *seen* me before, for God's sake —"

"But that's impossible! I mean, how *could* he?"

Belinda shook her head miserably. "That's what I've been trying to tell you — *nothing* makes sense. He *couldn't* have seen me any other place except the crash. Who knows where he could have been lying around there, and we didn't even notice him — we just ran off and left him there —"

"We didn't know!" Hildy's voice rose nervously. "If we'd known about him, then we'd have helped him. Stop doing this, Belinda; you're scaring me!"

"I'm scaring *you?*" Belinda's look was incredulous. "Someone's been giving me warnings and leaving sick things around my house, and tonight someone came after me in the park. I can't go to the police — after what happened the other day, they're already suspicious of me! I can't even tell my mother, and my best friends won't take me seriously —"

"But — *still* — we can't be *sure* —"

"Sure? Hildy, it was the same road — how much of a coincidence can *that* be?" She paused as Hildy shook her head. "If Adam wants revenge . . ."

"I don't want to talk about this anymore, okay?"

"So you're going to pretend there's no danger? It hasn't been happening to you, so you're just going to write it off?" Belinda suppressed a sudden urge to shake some sense into her, and then she saw the look on Hildy's face. "But you really are scared, too, aren't you?"

"I don't want to talk about this anymore. I came over to hear about Noel and to talk about the picnic."

Belinda groaned and threw up her hands. "The picnic. Okay, you win . . . even though you know *I'm* not going to —"

"Whoops, there's the bell!" Hildy jumped up, obviously relieved to have the unpleasant discussion at an end. She raced to the door and jerked it open. "Okay, get your tastebuds all set for —"

"Hi. Is Belinda here?"

" — some guy," Hildy finished. "Who are you?"

"Who is it?" Alarm rose in Belinda, and she was halfway off the couch when she saw the tall boy step into the house. "Noel! What are you doing here?" Helplessly she glanced around at the messy living room, the dirty dishes sitting on the end tables, the clutter. *Too late now . . . he's already seen what a slob I am.*

"I know I just saw you," he said almost shyly. Hildy was just standing there gaping at him, and he looked away, embarrassed.

"No — that's okay. Come in. Sit down." Belinda started to clear some magazines off a chair, then noticed that Hildy had her back to them and was staring out the door. "Hildy, you can shut the door now —"

"I wanted to talk to you," Noel began, "but if you're busy —"

"Pizza," Belinda said. "We're just waiting for pizza and — Hildy, will you please shut the door?"

"There's someone out there," Hildy whispered.

"What?" Belinda was instantly alert, and as Hildy backed into the room, she crept to the curtains at the window and tried to peer out. "Turn off the lights, Hildy! Shut that door!"

While Noel looked on in dismay, Hildy slammed the door and hit the light switch, crowding in close to Belinda.

"I don't see anything," Belinda mumbled. "Are you positive — ?"

"Yes! He was right out there on the sidewalk!"

"Where? What was he doing?"

"Just standing there looking at the house. Look — oh, God — there he is —"

"Where?" Belinda's voice raised, and as her eyes scanned the darkness of the lawn, a stealthy movement drew her eyes to the shrubbery near the drive-way. "Oh . . . Noel . . ."

"What is it?" And Noel was already opening the

door, starting down the walk, even as Belinda grabbed for him, pulling him back.

"It's too late, Noel — he's gone —"

"Gone? But did you get a good look at him?"

"Yes." Belinda stared at him as he shut the door . . . stared at Hildy as she gazed back with wide, scared eyes. "Yes," she said again, and this time a laugh bubbled up, nervous and more than a little incredulous. "It . . . it looked like Cobbs."

"Cobbs!" Noel was looking at her as if she'd just sprouted three heads. "Belinda, are you serious?"

But he parted the curtains and peered out into the night.

And suddenly he wasn't smiling anymore.

Chapter 11

"It was probably just someone taking a walk," Hildy said quickly. "Oh, come on, Belinda, whoever it was just stopped to think or catch his breath or something —"

Belinda gave a small nod. "Probably. . . ."

Noel glanced back at them over his shoulder. "Things look so different in the dark — shadows can play tricks with your eyes." He turned from the window and sighed. "And anyway, what possible reason would Cobbs have for lurking around in the dark? If he *did* have some reason for coming here to your house, he'd come to the door and ring the bell —" Noel paused, throwing Belinda a half-amused look. "He's funny about manners that way."

In spite of her nervousness, Hildy snickered, immediately catching a glare from Belinda. "Uh . . . I'll watch for the food," Hildy said, and promptly went out onto the porch, closing the door behind her.

"Belinda, why do I get the feeling there's more going on here than I know about?" Noel came up quietly to her side. "Will you please tell me what's —"

"Nothing." Belinda smiled. "It's nothing. We were telling ghost stories when you came — we scared ourselves, that's all." She hadn't fooled him, and she knew it. "Come on and sit down. The pizza should be here any minute."

The look on Noel's face was still wary, but he took a chair while Belinda perched on the arm of the couch.

"I was worried about you," Noel said. "I just wanted to make sure you were okay."

"I'm okay. Really."

"Ever since I brought you home, I've just been driving around . . . thinking about Adam. And thinking maybe you should know some things —"

Belinda glanced up apprehensively. "What kinds of things?"

"Things I've heard . . . things that might help you understand him — if Adam can ever be understood." He looked uncomfortable, almost guilty, and Belinda felt sorry for him. "I don't like repeating things like this — that's how vicious rumors get started — and Adam's not here to give his side."

"Can I ask where you heard them from?"

A reluctant nod. "My mom. And Fred, too. But they're — I mean — how could they *really* know Adam? How could *anybody* really know Adam?"

Belinda nodded. "All right — I get what you're saying."

Noel paused, then shoved his hands deep in his pockets, angling himself stiffly back in his chair.

"Adam has a history of . . . well . . . imagining things."

"What does that mean exactly?"

"It means that sometimes he makes things up or . . . thinks things happen that really don't. Fred told me himself a long time ago. That Adam was always in trouble. That Adam always had a chip on his shoulder. That Adam was a compulsive liar. Fred blamed himself — for running out on him when Adam really needed a father."

"It sounds like people have been running out on Adam all his life," Belinda said gloomily.

"I guess he's been hurt a lot. So he acts tough to protect himself. Like . . . I'll hurt you first so you can't ever hurt me . . . something like that."

Belinda sighed and sprawled back against the cushions.

"Anyway," Noel went on, "I guess now he's having this — I don't know — delusion — that somebody else caused this car accident he was in and —"

"Caused . . ." As Belinda tried to speak, every nerve jolted, the room swaying around her. "What . . . did you say?"

". . . Adam says someone tried to run him off the road." Noel was speaking, but she heard him distantly, down a long dark tunnel of fear. ". . . has nightmares about it."

Belinda stared, her lips moving soundlessly.

". . . don't know where he gets these things in his head — hey, are you okay?"

"Yes. Yes, I'm fine." *Smile, Belinda.* "Poor Adam. I'm just so sorry —"

"And it's so obvious he just missed the curve and went off the road — of course Mom can't remember much of anything — with all the pills she had in her when it happened." He shook his head. "She always dopes herself up when she has to fly —"

Belinda tried to stand up but her body wouldn't move.

"Anyway . . ." Noel's voice sank apologetically, "if Adam seems more weird than usual, he's been through a hell of a lot. And . . . well, if he's directing it all at you . . . maybe it's just because you're willing to listen to his feelings — none of the rest of us can stand to be around him."

This time she managed to heave herself out of her chair. As she tried to stand, however, her foot snagged on the cushion and Noel caught her, just as Hildy and Frank came through the front door.

"Well, well, Belinda, don't let us interrupt — *oof!*" Frank doubled over as Hildy elbowed him in the stomach, and Noel released Belinda, blushing as they stared at him.

"I found him outside," Hildy gave a nervous smile, not sure about Belinda's reaction. "And he paid for the pizza, so what could I do?"

Belinda stood there stiffly, Frank's earlier behavior still painfully fresh in her mind.

"Well, aren't you gonna introduce us to your friend?" Frank grinned. He stuck out his hand and Noel shook it politely. "I'm Frank Scaleri. And if you're some new secret of Belinda's, she's kept it very well."

Noel smiled, the picture of courtesy. "Noel Ashby."

"I'm Hildy Crane." Hildy watched Noel's fingers close around her own. "I'm Belinda's best friend. And Frank's. Well — actually — we're all best friends."

"Nice to meet you, Hildy. Sorry to run out like this, but I really have to get back —"

"Uhhhh . . ." In one quick movement Hildy got between Noel and the door, while Belinda looked on in dismay. "Uhhh . . . Belinda . . . we really need to talk about the picnic."

"Yes. The picnic." Frank nodded vigorously. "The good ole senior picnic. Yes, indeed."

Belinda was staring at them in shock. She could feel her cheeks beginning to burn. "We can talk about it later —"

"But the . . . uh . . . numbers!" Hildy piped up, a triumphant smile on her face. "We have to know how many are going! Do you have a date yet, Belinda?"

Belinda was absolutely mortified. As she glared at Hildy, Noel looked at each of them in turn, and a slow smile spread over his face.

"And what picnic is this?" he asked graciously.

Belinda pleaded with her eyes, but Hildy rushed on. "Our senior picnic. It's gonna be in the park — and it's gonna be so much fun — they're gonna have a band and —"

"Yeah, Noel, do you like picnics?" Frank asked with exaggerated casualness.

"I love picnics," Noel looked amused. "And I'd love to take you, Belinda, if you don't already have a date."

"She doesn't." Hildy shook her head. "And she'd love to go with you, wouldn't you, Belinda?"

Noel looked like he was really struggling now not to laugh. He cocked his head at Belinda and said, "After all the trouble they went to, the least you could do is say yes."

"I . . . yes . . . but you —"

"You can give me the details tomorrow." Noel said as Hildy stepped away from the door. "*Now* can I go?"

"Of course," Hildy grinned.

Noel turned back to Belinda, a hint of worry beneath his smile. "I hope . . . everything's okay."

"Yes." Belinda stared after him, aching to tell him, knowing she couldn't. "Thanks."

The door closed and she sank numbly back onto the couch. Frank took the pizza into the kitchen. Hildy leaned against the door with a smile and played with the tips of her braids. Making sure Frank was out of earshot, she hissed, "So *that's* Noel. God, is he cute! You are so *lucky!*"

"I'm lucky?" Belinda squeezed her eyes shut and put one arm across her face.

Hildy stood there uncertainly, waiting for Belinda to look up. When she didn't, Hildy took a hesitant step toward the couch.

"I did it for your own good. You'd never have done it on your own."

Belinda didn't answer.

"I didn't *beg*, you know. He asked you all by himself."

Belinda pressed one hand to her swollen cheek. She felt too exhausted to argue. "Adam thinks someone tried to run him off the road."

"What?" Hildy's smile locked strangely on her lips.

"Everyone else thinks the car just missed the curve — but Adam says the accident wasn't his fault. And Adam imagines things, so no one believes him."

Hildy's breath came out in a rush. "Then what are you worried about? And anyway — you *still* can't be sure it's the same —"

"I'm going to bed." Belinda got up and started down the hall, leaving Hildy staring open-mouthed.

"But, Belinda — I thought we were going to talk!"

"Talk to Frank."

Hildy only looked crushed for a moment. As she heard Belinda's bedroom door close, she yelled, "You're really crazy, you know that?" And then, as her mind flashed back to Noel and the picnic, she looked smug and very pleased with herself. "Okay," she called to the bedroom door, "but someday, Belinda Swanson, you'll thank me for this!"

". . . *so obvious he just missed the curve*" . . . "*thinks things happen that really don't . . .*"

Sighing, Belinda pillowed her head on folded arms and stared out her window into the night. She couldn't remember ever feeling so utterly alone . . . so deeply afraid. She didn't know what to do. She didn't know what was happening. She just lay there, eyes fixed on her window, on the shadows framed and hung against the sky.

She thought of Adam. Adam choking on hate and anger — hiding in his dark room in a dark, cruel world where nobody cared. Belinda felt sick and hopeless inside. *Is this how Adam feels? Like nothing will ever get any better? Like no one will ever —*

Her breath caught in her throat.

Across from the foot of her bed, the open window suddenly darkened and filled.

In some remote part of her terrified brain, she tried to believe that a cloud had simply swept over the moon, swathing the room in darkness.

But deep inside . . . in the deepest part of her . . . Belinda knew better.

She knew that the hulking shape in the window was real.

As real as the soft, slow scraping of human hands across the screen . . .

In slow motion Belinda sat up, her eyes glued in horrible fascination on the person framed there in her window.

She couldn't see his face.

But she felt his eyes.

And she heard his voice.

Low and harsh and full of the worst dangers —
"Murderer," he hissed. *"Murderer."*

And then the soft flow of moonlight spread over
the bed once more . . .

And the window was empty.

Chapter 12

"You were dreaming," Hildy said again.

"No." Belinda looked terrible, deep circles around her sleepless eyes . . . a listlessness that made her seem frail. "I wasn't."

"We both looked last night, didn't we? No footprints. Nothing." Hildy pulled her close in a quick hug. "Hey, come on, don't go back there to see Adam. You're killing yourself."

"I have to go back — I have to know the truth — " Belinda shook her head, not trusting herself to speak, and let her gaze wander up the street.

"You're getting a ride, I hope," Hildy admonished. "You're not going on the bus, right?"

"Cobbs is supposed to pick me up any minute — but, Hildy —"

"What now?"

"What time did Frank leave last night?"

"Oh, I don't know, about —" Hildy broke off, her look suspicious. "Okay, Belinda, I see your mind working — you think Frank was prowling around the house, peeping in windows, just 'cause he left before I did —"

"I didn't say that."

"But you were thinking it." Hildy looked annoyed. "Aren't you getting kinda tired of blaming Frank for everything?"

"Me? What about you? You're the one who's always saying it's Frank playing all these stupid jokes —"

"Well, maybe it was your friend Cobbs —"

"Cobbs wouldn't go around spying in windows —"

"Right. Just hiding in bushes. I don't suppose it's ever occurred to you that maybe you could have *imagined* —"

"There's my ride." Relieved, Belinda saw Noel's red car pull to the curb, Sasha hanging out the window, all wags and kisses.

"And don't forget the picnic!" Hildy called. "If you don't have a nervous breakdown before then!"

As Belinda climbed into the front, Noel gave her a concerned smile.

"Hi there — you recovered?"

"Sure. Down below all these cuts and bruises, I actually have a face." She tried to laugh.

"And that face is actually perfect." Noel's eyes twinkled. "And what was that deliberate reminder about the picnic I just heard?"

"Look . . . Noel . . ." Belinda shifted to face him. "Hildy loves to interfere, and I'm really sorry —"

"Sorry for what? If it hadn't been for her, I'd have never known about the picnic, and I'd still be working up my nerve to ask you out."

Belinda lowered her head, smiling. "Thank you. I really do appreciate it, but —"

"But nothing — we have a date. And I hope you won't break it, because I'll probably be inconsolable if you do. So please don't hurt my feelings."

In spite of herself, Belinda laughed. "Okay. I won't hurt your feelings."

"Hear that, Sasha?" Noel spoke into the rearview mirror, and the dog gave a loud bark. "That's why Sasha's my best girl," Noel confided, "because she never rejects me."

"I understand." Belinda laughed again, and this time it felt surprisingly good.

Noel dropped her off at the house, explaining he had errands to run, but promised to be back to take her home again. Cobbs looked up from his dusting as she lingered in the entryway.

"Ready for battle, miss?"

"Not really." Her eyes went slowly around the living room, over the glass boxes. The cloths were off today, and she could see coiled bodies everywhere . . . exploring their see-through walls . . . probing the glass with their quick tongues . . . as if they sensed a new presence in the room.

"Cobbs?"

"Yes, miss."

"The weirdest thing happened last night — I thought I saw you."

For just a split second, his rigid back seemed to go straighter. As Belinda stared, the dust rag went round and round in neat concentric circles, but the white head remained bowed, concentrated on his work.

"I, miss?"

"Yes, in front of my house. I know it couldn't have been you, but it was so strange — it really *looked* like you."

"Forgive me, miss, but it couldn't have been I. . . ." Cobbs's eyes shifted upward in a sidelong glance. "Now, could it?"

"No . . . no, I guess not." Belinda glanced again at the snakes in their boxes and gave a shudder. "Why aren't they covered today?"

"They're due for an airing out."

"*Ugh*. How can you even stand to be around them?"

Cobbs raised an eyebrow. "Why do you think I carry a cleaver?"

It made Belinda smile, and she felt a little more reassured as she let herself into Adam's room. He was standing in his usual spot in the corner, and Belinda went resolutely to the window and raised the shade. *Two can play this game, Adam. . . .*

"We don't need it dark in here anymore," she said.

Adam glowered but made no move to stop her as she turned on the lamp and looked at him. His body was tall and lean in jeans and a sweatshirt. His soft, thick hair curled slightly over his collar, and his eyes were watchful . . . as watchful as those that had stared back at her from their cages downstairs.

"Why do you keep coming back here, Belinda

Swanson?" Adam asked coolly. "I must be so fascinating to you."

Deliberately, Belinda turned her back on him, trying not to tremble as she took off her jacket and started sorting through a stack of books.

"Curiosity killed the cat, you know," Adam sounded amused. "How's your face?"

Belinda glanced at him sharply, but he was gazing out the window. "It's fine," she said, choosing a book and turning the pages. "How're your legs today?"

"You can quit playing soulmate. We're nothing alike."

"Well," Belinda replied, "thank God for that."

The glance Adam threw her was almost surprised. She sat down and thrust the book out at him.

"Here. You might as well show me where you left off, so I can get to work. We've wasted enough time already."

If her manner really did surprise him, he was careful not to show it. Belinda sat in silence, watching him flip slowly through the text, watching his slender fingers brush lightly . . . methodically . . . over the pages.

"So Noel's taking you to your picnic," Adam mumbled.

Belinda paused, forcing her voice calm. "Did Noel tell you that?"

"Noel doesn't have to tell me. I just know." The fingers stopped. The room was quiet. "Noel doesn't tell me anything. Noel and I don't talk at all."

Belinda didn't know what to say. She shifted nervously and hoped Adam wouldn't notice.

"I had a girlfriend once," Adam said slowly. He turned one page . . . hesitated . . . turned another. "She cheated on me. Behind my back."

Belinda gripped the edge of her seat, and kept her face impassive.

"She had . . . an accident. Freaky thing, really." He shrugged. "Oh, well . . . nobody goes out with her now."

"So is that supposed to scare me?" Belinda gazed back at him, deliberately meeting those black, black eyes. "Your book," she said tightly. "How far have you gotten?"

"Aren't you sorry about my girlfriend, Belinda?" Adam gave her a slow smile.

"Yes."

"You didn't say so."

"I'm sorry about your girlfriend."

"And my face . . . all these scars —"

"I'm sorry about your face."

"Strange . . . you don't *seem* sorry."

She grabbed for the book in his hand but he snatched it back, and as she fell against him, his arm locked around her neck.

"Funny thing about accidents." Adam's lips moved against her ear. "You never know when they might happen."

Belinda jerked free, her heart racing. "If you have something to say to me, just say it, Adam." She whirled away from him, slammed her books together, and whipped her jacket from the desk.

"What's that?" Adam's voice stopped her. She spun back around, bewildered. He was pointing at something on the floor by her feet, and she followed his look, choking down a cry.

It was the bloodstained handkerchief.

Somehow it had fallen out of her pocket and landed, splayed out on the floor, its torn A showing on top.

Belinda gazed down at it, feeling deathly ill.

"It's mine." Quickly she snatched it up and jammed it back in her pocket, her hands shaking so violently she knew he couldn't miss it.

Adam was staring at her.

"It's mine," she said again. "I keep it . . . 'cause I get nosebleeds."

With deliberate slowness his eyes raised to her face, and she fought to keep it expressionless.

"I'm not coming here again," she was backing toward the door, dropping her purse, fumbling to pick it up. "If your stepmother wants a tutor, she'll have to get somebody else."

"Where'd you get it?" Adam asked calmly.

"What? This? I told you, it's mine!" Behind her, Belinda found the doorknob. The door was stuck, and she yanked on it. "I found it, and it belongs to me." *Oh, God, no, I really didn't say that, did I?*

She slammed his door and hurried down the stairs. She could hear his cane . . . his foot dragging across the floor —

"Cobbs! Cobbs, are you here?" She came breathlessly into the kitchen as Cobbs glanced up from the sink. His sleeves were rolled neatly past his elbows, and he was soaping off dirt and grease from his hands. Belinda made a split second effort to compose herself. "Cobbs — please can you take me home now?"

"Normally I'd jump at the chance," Cobbs frowned. "Unfortunately, the car seems to be temporarily indisposed."

"But I can't wait. Isn't Noel back yet?"

Cobbs's look swept the empty kitchen. "Yes. He's invisible."

Belinda tried to hold her impatience in check. "I'll just call a cab, if that's okay. You wouldn't happen to know the number, would you?"

"In the exhilaration of the moment, it escapes me."

Belinda went over to the phone and lifted the receiver, then jumped as she heard a voice on the other end.

"I'm sorry, but there's no change."

The voice sounded brusque, businesslike, someone Belinda didn't recognize. Embarrassed, she started to replace the receiver when Adam's deep voice spoke out on the line.

"No change at all? Nothing?"

"No, sir —"

"And he hasn't regained consciousness — he hasn't said *anything* —"

"No sir, not a word, we're just —"

"Well, can't you do something?"

"We're doing all we can, we —"

"To hurry it along, I mean. To put him out of his misery — how long does he have to linger like that?

How long do the rest of us have to suffer through this —"

"Sir . . . I'm very sorry . . . but as I've told you —"

Belinda eased the phone down, her heart pounding sickeningly in her chest.

But not before hearing one last exchange.

"So he really is going to die? You're positive about that?"

"As the doctor's told you — *many* times — there's absolutely no hope. It's only a matter of waiting."

"Waiting," Adam murmured. "Waiting, waiting, and we're still waiting. . . ."

There was a click as the nurse hung up.

And then Adam made a sound — *a cry? a laugh?* — that sent shivers through Belinda's soul.

"No more waiting," Adam whispered. "We've waited long enough."

Chapter 13

"All set for the picnic?" Hildy linked her arm through Belinda's as they strolled slowly across campus. Already buses were lined up to transport eager seniors to the park, and those lucky enough to have cars were heading for the student lot, volunteering rides. Hildy spotted Frank beside his own car and waved. "Is Noel picking you up, Belinda?"

"No, he's going to meet me there. He wanted to stop by the hospital this morning."

"Then come with us. You don't want to ride with the rest of the rubble."

"That's rabble." Belinda laughed. "And it's nice to know what you think about your classmates."

"Hey, Belinda — how's the neurosis?" Frank grinned. "Any new ones we should be aware of?"

Hildy punched him on the chest and tried to look stern. "Frank — that's enough, okay? You're really going stale on us here."

"I'll find another ride," Belinda said quickly, but Frank grabbed her arm and steered her into the backseat.

"Okay, I'll do penance, I promise. Fifty lashes with Hildy's tongue — or would *you* like to volunteer?"

"Oh, please —"

"Okay, I give up! You two are so touchy today!" He climbed in and slammed his door. "I sure hope this picnic puts you in a better mood. And if you don't mind me saying so, Belinda, you look like hell."

"Thanks for the compliment," she retorted and Hildy held up her hands.

"*Wait* a minute here. What is *happening* to us? We used to get along so well —"

"Ask Miss High and Mighty," Frank grunted. "Hanging around with the *wealthy* set now, maybe she's too good for us —"

"I'm just a lowly tutor," Belinda reminded him. "Just one of the help."

"Yeah, well, I wish it'd help your attitude —"

"*My* attitude? Look, I'm not the one who's been —"

"Just forget it, okay, Belinda? I can't take all the craziness anymore. So let's just stay out of each other's way, and when you decide to join the human race again —"

"Stop it!" Hildy covered her ears and glared from one to the other. "Frank, just let up, okay? And Belinda, just don't listen to him." She smiled, settling back. "And then we'll all be happy. See how easy it is?"

Belinda closed her eyes and leaned her head against the car window, not speaking again until they got to the park. While Frank pulled Hildy off to join the others, she stood there, watching all the familiar faces mingle for one of the last times. It was strange, how she'd never felt particularly close to any of them — yet now a lump formed in her throat as she realized she'd probably never see most of them again. Suddenly she wished she'd taken the time to know them better . . . to socialize more . . . to make more friends. . . . And she thought of Adam, alone in the dark . . . and suddenly she wanted to tell Hildy how much she meant to her, in spite of all that had happened these last few weeks.

"You're looking pretty sentimental," a voice said gently and Noel was there beside her, smiling as if he understood.

"Well . . . you know." Belinda laughed self-consciously and waved as Hildy yelled hello in the distance. "Senior-itis, as my mom would say."

"Is that all?"

She glanced up and shook her head slowly. "No. That's not all."

"Somehow I didn't think it was. Come on."

Noel took her hand and led her through the crowds. All around them kids were laughing and shouting, radio music blaring from loudspeakers, the air filled with the smoky fragrance of barbecue. As they followed the pathways through the park, Noel spotted a bench beside a fountain and they sat down, the noise and activity fading behind them.

"You seemed kind of upset when I got back to the house last night." Noel propped himself against an ivy-covered wall. "You hardly said a word on the way home."

"It was Adam," Belinda admitted. *And that phone call. . . .*

"What happened?"

"Oh, he started acting scary again. Just saying things like he was trying to upset me. But it was the way he looked. The way he talked. Like he was really enjoying it."

"He probably was. Look, Belinda . . . Adam enjoys upsetting people. It gives him control over them." Noel looked thoughtful for a minute, his voice sank low. "I don't think he's had much control over his own life."

Belinda sighed. "I guess you're right. At least when my parents split up, somebody wanted me."

"Yes." His soft eyes went slowly across the path and settled on a small brown sparrow. "That's very important, isn't it? To be wanted? To be loved?"

Belinda watched him, feeling sorry somehow, but not sure why. "You've always been loved, haven't you?"

Noel thought a while. "As much as my mom's capable of loving, I guess. She doesn't love me as much as she loves herself — or money" — he broke into a slow grin — "but I guess I run a close third."

Belinda laughed. "Well, does she love Fred?"

Noel nodded, his face growing serious. "Fred's been good to her — *and* to me. One thing you have to understand, Belinda — when you've never had money — and then you get it — it's sort of like an addiction. You want more and more. . . ." His eyes dropped, and he stared hard at a sunspot on the bench, "and you can't ever imagine being without it again. And that" — he roused himself and gave her a sly wink — "explains my mother. Thank God *I* don't live with her."

Belinda smiled into his eyes as he took her hand. "What happened to your dad?"

"He divorced her, smart man."

"Do you still see him?"

"No, he died when I was thirteen."

"I'm sorry."

"Don't be. He had a happy life. Especially after he left my mother."

"Hey, you two, aren't you gonna eat?"

They looked up as Hildy appeared, her plate overflowing with food. She smiled winningly at Noel and then eased herself down onto the bench beside them.

"Isn't this great? The band's setting up now — food and music all day long!"

"Where's Frank?" Belinda peered off into the distant crowds. "Still being a jerk?"

"Oh . . ." Hildy looked uncomfortable, shrugging her shoulders. "You know Frank, he'll get over it. If you'd just . . . well . . . you know. . . ."

Belinda chose to ignore the hint and stood up, brushing off the seat of her jeans. "Come on — I guess we'd better go stand in line."

"You know, I'm really glad you volunteered for this." Hildy brightened, beaming at Noel. "She needs someone to take care of her."

Noel grinned at Belinda's discomfiture. "She seems pretty capable to me, but I promise I'll keep my eye on her."

"That's a load off my mind." Hildy smiled sweetly and Noel returned it, steering Belinda away from them and back toward the crowds.

"Interesting friends you have." He grinned.

"Yeah . . . well . . ." Belinda shrugged apologetically. "They like to give me a hard time."

"I've noticed. You hang out a lot together?"

"All the time —" Belinda caught herself. "Well, *most* of the time. I try not to be a tagalong."

Noel chuckled. "I understand. You're lucky to have close friends, though. At boarding school, they all live too far away once school's out."

"And maybe we live too *close* sometimes." Belinda laughed. "We get on each other's nerves."

"Well then, it's my pleasure to rescue you."

Belinda took a deep breath and stepped back. "Noel . . . you got trapped into this today, and I'm very embarrassed about it."

"You should be," Noel said solemnly. "Just before the picnic, Frank threatened me, and I had to come."

"Noel, I'm serious!" Belinda tried not to laugh, and Noel's arms went around her, resting lightly on her waist.

"I know you are. And so am I. I wanted to come. I wanted to be with you. Simple as that. End of discussion."

"But —"

"No arguments. I'm too hungry to argue. Let's eat instead."

"All right . . . but be prepared for all kinds of stares and introductions," Belinda warned him.

And he was smiling down at her, and she was laughing, and suddenly she really *did* feel hungry . . . and happy.

Belinda couldn't believe how quickly the afternoon flew by. She couldn't even remember when she had smiled so much and laughed so hard. Today there were no worries — only cool sunshine and the comforting joy of the people around her, and the special closeness of Noel. She was surprised at how much fun she was actually having just because he was with her — and how he seemed to be enjoying himself just as much.

As twilight fell and the band broke up, the crowds finally began heading homeward beneath a crisp, starless sky. Belinda was out of breath from laughing as she and Noel helped score their volleyball team's winning point, and he took her hand, lifting it to his lips for a victory kiss.

"Does this mean we have to leave?" he asked, watching their teammates drift away, waving goodbye.

"No . . . we could just walk around in the dark for a while till you get tired."

"Cute. Real cute. Well, just because the picnic's over doesn't mean *we* have to be. Know any good restaurants?"

"Still hungry?" Belinda laughed. "You are so crazy —"

"No, *Adam's* crazy. You and I are the sane ones, remember?"

The mention of Adam sobered her a little. They walked along side by side, and then suddenly Noel caught her close in a quick hug.

"Belinda . . . you are really something."

She felt warm inside as he smiled down at her, his fingers brushing her hair. It seemed natural to slip her arm around his waist . . . natural that they fit together so perfectly. And then, as he slowly tilted her chin, his lips closed gently over hers.

Belinda felt lost in the breathlessness of the moment. When she opened her eyes again, Noel was watching her, a thoughtful smile on his face.

"It was all a plot," he mumbled, shaking his head. "The *volleyball* games, the *softball* games, the *dancing*, not to mention all the *chaperones* — all that just to keep me from kissing you — God, Belinda, a simple 'no' would have done the trick —"

"Oh, you!" Belinda aimed a punch at his arm, but he caught her hand easily and laughed, pressing it to his lips.

"I liked that kiss," she said shyly.

"Yeah?" Noel teased and unlocked the car, giving her a shove into the front seat. "Well, if you *must* know, so did I."

Since Noel decided nothing would satisfy his hunger pains except Mexican food, Belinda suggested a favorite restaurant outside of town. The popular place was overflowing with Friday night crowds. After a lengthy wait for a table, Belinda tried to concentrate on her enchiladas but was uncomfortably aware of Noel staring at her.

"Don't watch me. I can't eat if you're watching me."

"I like to watch you. You look nice in this soft light."

"The light's bad, and your eyes are bad. Quit looking at me."

"I don't want to quit looking at you. And as a matter of fact, I *shouldn't* quit looking at you, since I'm supposed to be taking care of you."

Belinda shook her head, remembering Noel's promise to Hildy. "I don't need to be taken care of. I can take care of myself."

"I'm not so sure about that." Noel grinned. His leg brushed hers under the table, and Belinda flushed, catching his wink before she looked away.

The sky was still overcast when they got back in the car. For a few moments they sat there, staring out the windshield, Belinda's head on his shoulder. The breeze was chilly and damp, and a thin fog had begun to swirl along the ground.

"I don't want to take you home," Noel said reluctantly. "It's been such a perfect day —"

"After you got roped into it," Belinda teased.

"Hey — I thought we settled that." He tried to look stern but ended up smiling instead. "Will anyone be there at your house? I don't want to just drop you off there alone —"

"I'm always alone. It's okay."

"You're making me feel unchivalrous. Maybe I should just stay."

"Oh. My mother would *love* that."

"Okay." He gave an exaggerated sigh and pulled out onto the road. "But at least let me come in and look around before I leave you there."

She nodded and sank back against him, his right arm curled protectively around her shoulder as he drove. From time to time she could feel his cheek nestled against her hair, and she closed her eyes, drifting in a safe, happy glow.

The crash snapped her forward without warning.

Blinking her eyes in confusion, she felt Noel's arm tighten around her — heard his angry, stunned voice as he pushed her back onto her own side —

"Whoa, what the hell's this guy —"

Something rammed them from behind.

Belinda gasped and flung out her hands, grateful for the seat belt that held her in place.

"What's happening?" she cried, yet in her deepest fears she knew what was happening — because it had happened once before —

"This guy's crazy!" Noel yelled. He sounded scared, and Belinda's own fear threatened to choke her. "Hang on — I'm going to try and outrun him —"

Oh, God . . . oh, God . . . this time it'll be me . . . and Noel. . . .

She gasped as Noel gunned the engine, as the car shot forward, flinging her back against the seat. She tried to turn around . . . to see the driver face to face. . . .

The car had no headlights.

She screamed as they skidded around a curve . . . slid over the foggy wetness of a one-lane bridge. The car jerked with another ram from behind. The tires screeched and the darkness was everywhere and Noel was muttering something under his breath that she couldn't make out —

They flew over a pothole — sailed several feet into the air —

Belinda saw the barbed wire fence . . . the ditch beyond —

She clamped her eyes shut and braced herself.

The car jolted to a stop.

For an eternity Belinda sat there, pinned by deep, empty silence, paralyzed with stark, icy terror. Then finally she felt herself breathe again . . . felt her eyes move slowly to Noel.

At first she thought he was dead.

He was slumped against his door, and he wasn't moving.

"Noel — oh, my God —" Her hands fumbled with her seat belt, and she saw him raise his head. Blood ran in a thin trickle over one eye. "Oh, Noel, you're hurt!"

"I'm all right." His voice was shaky . . . and very cold. "What about you?"

"I'm fine —"

"Sure? You can move everything?"

"Yes — yes! Let's hurry and get out of here —"

"The maniac already passed me. Damn . . . I don't believe this . . . my car —"

"I think it was Adam," Belinda said.

"*Adam?*" Noel stared at her, his mouth open, as if he didn't know whether to laugh or get her a doctor. "*Adam?*" he repeated numbly. "Adam can't drive a car . . . Adam can't even *walk!* How the hell could it have been Adam?"

"I don't know. But I think it was."

Noel pulled back from her, stiffly, against his door. "Belinda, what is *with* you?" Anger flooded his voice now, his eyes, every feature — even through the pale shock of his face she could see it. "What *is* this thing with Adam, anyway? It's like you're . . . you're obsessed with him or something! I'm sorry I even told you anything about him — you're seeing him in every shadow!"

"No — you don't understand —"

"No. I *don't* understand."

Belinda tried to shut out the hurt in his voice. "Noel — I can't explain it now, but I think he's after me — I don't know how, but —"

Noel was shaking his head, mouthing "no" over and over again, but as Belinda's panic grew, he suddenly reached out and caught her shoulders. "Okay, Belinda, okay. Whatever this is about, I think you'd better tell me."

Tears filled her eyes, and she nodded. "Yes."

He searched her face, his own sad and bewildered. "You shouldn't be alone at your house tonight."

"No," she whispered.

After several moments he released her and tried the key. Belinda saw his hands were shaking. The car made a grinding noise, but finally backed up onto the road.

"We'll call your mother from my place," Noel said tiredly. "I'll tell her you got sick and Cobbs put you to bed."

Belinda stared out at the road, her voice tight. "But I don't want to go there. Adam will be there."

"Belinda" — Noel glanced over, his hand reaching again for her shoulder — "Adam's not even home right now. . . ."

And as Belinda stared at him in slow disbelief, he added softly, "It's Cobbs's night off. He and Adam went out somewhere together."

Chapter 14

They didn't talk on the way home.

Belinda sank into a mild stupor, wondering how the perfect day had gone so wrong, and beside her Noel clung to the wheel, his eyes going frequently to the rearview mirror. There were no more mishaps, and when Sasha greeted them joyously at the door, they hugged her between themselves, as if she were some solid link of sanity. Noel called the hospital, explaining to Belinda's mother that she'd gotten ill and Cobbs had insisted on keeping her, and Mrs. Swanson thanked them both for their caring. As Noel hung up the phone, he regarded Belinda with obvious concern, and suggested they call it a night.

"I wasn't lying to your mother, you know — you really do look sick."

"You don't look too good yourself."

"Oh, don't worry about me." He brushed her off. "But are you okay? Really?"

She avoided his eyes. "Do you . . . still want to talk?"

"I think we should. If you're up to it."

"Are you *sure* Adam isn't here?"

Noel reached for the coffeemaker, then hesitated, casting a glance at her over his shoulder. "He's not here. I told you, he's with Cobbs. I think they were going to the movies."

"Adam couldn't have — you know — changed his mind?"

"Would it make you feel better if I went to the theater and saw him for myself?"

Belinda flushed. She felt so stupid . . . so angry with herself, yet she couldn't help it. "Could you just . . . check the house?"

Noel smiled then. He set the coffee down and guided her out of the kitchen. "I'll do better than that. I'll personally show you to your room, and *you* can lock your door, and *then* I'll check the house."

He led her down another upstairs hallway to a cozy room at the back of the house. While Belinda looked around, he excused himself for a minute, and by the time she had found a bathroom and some towels, he had reappeared, carrying a white, silky nightgown.

"Mom's," he apologized. "It'll probably be too long . . . but I'm sure it'll look better on you than it does on her."

Belinda tried to imagine Mrs. Thorne in one of her own flannel nightgowns but couldn't quite conjure up the image. She sat down on the edge of the four-poster bed as Noel drew the curtains and showed her empty hangers in the closet.

"And if you need anything at all, just yell."

"I will," Belinda said nervously. "Is your room close by?"

"Two doors down. And Cobbs is off the kitchen, but if you need a snack or anything just pound on his door."

"I won't need anything," Belinda said softly.

"Belinda —" Noel took a step toward her, his face worried. "Look, I know you're tired, but —"

"Could we talk tomorrow?" she turned away. "I know I said I'd tell you but . . ."

Noel seemed to be having a mental struggle. At last he said, "Okay, I'll see you in the morning," and she heard the door close quietly behind him.

Belinda lay back with a sigh, so overwhelmed with fears and questions, she couldn't even think. It took all her effort to get ready for bed. She slipped the sheer nightgown over her head, the white silk smooth and cool against her skin. She looked at herself in the full-length mirror, somewhat amazed at the transformation. Her brown hair fell gently over the tiny straps at her shoulders, and the low-cut front was trimmed in soft lace, hugging the curves of her body. Mrs. Thorne must have paid a small fortune for this nightgown, and Belinda guessed the woman wouldn't be a bit happy to know it had been loaned out. Still . . . it made her feel almost pretty, and Belinda looked at her reflection, smiling sadly at the stranger who smiled back.

She didn't hear the door open behind her.

She didn't see the tall shadow slip into the room until his reflection appeared in the mirror with hers.

"Noel!" Whirling around, Belinda crossed her

arms over her chest, her cheeks flaming hot as Noel took a startled step back.

"Hey — sorry, I didn't mean to scare you. I knocked . . . you forgot to lock your door. . . ." His voice trailed away as his eyes moved over her slowly, from her soft hair to her bare feet.

"I didn't hear you," Belinda murmured. She stood there, helplessly, so conscious of his eyes . . . so conscious of his nearness and the smile upon his face.

"Belinda. . . ." His lips moved gently, down her neck . . . his arms went around her, turning her to him, and as her body pressed against his, she could feel his heartbeat, as rapid as her own. She opened her eyes and he was looking down at her, brushing her hair back with his fingers.

"It suits you," he teased, and she blushed even more. "I think you should keep it — Mom'll never miss it."

Belinda tried to pull back, and his eyes lowered to the lace at her breasts. She pressed close to him again, feeling suddenly vulnerable.

"I . . . think I'd better go," Noel said at last, but as he released her, tears suddenly filled her eyes.

"Please don't leave," she said softly.

"Belinda, what is it? Are you crying?" And then as her body shook with sobs, he held her tightly. "What is it? Belinda . . . please tell me."

"I'm . . . I'm . . . so scared."

"Don't be — I'm here. Nothing's going to hurt you — please, Belinda — please tell me what's wrong —"

And she told him.

As he lowered her gently to the edge of the bed and they sat there in each other's arms, she sobbed out the whole horrible story — from the April Fools' Day party to Frank's joke — all the details of the wreck. She told him about the call to the police, about the calendar, the doll's head, the voice at her window. She told him everything — the whole series of nightmarish events that her life had become, and through it all Noel held her, rocked her, kept her safe. When she had finally exhausted herself, he went into the bathroom for tissues and began pacing while she blew her nose.

"But you really think Adam has something to do with all this?" he said at last, more than a little incredulous. "Even though he can't *walk* — even though the chances of that being the same *accident* are so — "

"Oh, Noel, I'm not sure of anything, but what other explanation is there?" Her voice rose desperately. "All those things I told you he said — he's been playing cat and mouse with me ever since I got here! But how could he know — *how?*"

"Could whoever it was have been lying somewhere nearby when you ran down the hill . . . didn't you say Hildy and Frank were yelling your name?"

"Yes . . . I suppose he could have heard them. And Hildy said some guy asked about me in the library — I don't know if it has any connection to this or not — but how did he *find* me? I'm so *scared*, Noel — I think he's trying to kill me!"

Noel held up his hands, palms outward. *"Whoa . . . now we're getting into serious business —"*

"It *is* serious business."

"And you haven't told anyone?"

"I can't. None of us were supposed to be out that night — Frank was drunk — and Hildy was driving! I can't do that to them —"

"Wait a minute." Noel shook his head slowly . . . walked to the window . . . walked back again. "What if it's something else?"

Belinda wiped her bleary eyes and sniffled. "What if *what's* something else?"

"The man." Noel cocked his head at her. "The man you said you saw on the hill —"

"The one they think I imagined —"

"Yes, but what if you *didn't* imagine him?" Noel's tone was tense; he knelt beside her, staring into her eyes. "Could *that* have been Adam?"

Belinda stared back at him, from beyond a throbbing headache.

"Suppose — just suppose Adam was up there watching you — hearing them call your name —"

"But — but Adam was in the wreck —"

"Adam *says* he was in the wreck." Noel frowned, his hand reaching for hers. "But what if he wasn't? What if he jumped out — or was thrown clear — and *that's* how he hurt himself?" His voice trailed off, and he shook his head. *"Listen* to me. I can't believe I'm standing here thinking all this stuff. I mean, why would he be so interested in you anyway, Belinda? Even if it *was* Adam, what possible reason could he have for wanting to hurt you?"

"Because I saw him." And suddenly it was so clear that her head spun with the impact of it all. "If Adam was up there, and the car was down there — with his father and stepmother inside — oh, God —"

Noel's glance was sharp. "I don't think I want to hear this, Belinda — stop —"

But in her mind, Belinda wasn't in the room anymore. She was down in the kitchen and it was the day before . . . and she was listening to Adam's conversation with a hospital nurse ". . . *he hasn't said anything . . . he really is going to die. . . .*"

"He tried to *kill* them, Noel! He tried to murder his own father — and *your* mother! But how — in the car — is that *possible*?"

Noel drew back, as if the very thought repelled him. But then, as Belinda continued to stare at him, he reluctantly shook his head. "It's not that hard to jump out of a car, I suppose — if you know what you're doing — but — still —"

"Why?" Belinda was almost begging now, trying to understand, horrified at the possibility. "Why would he try to kill them?"

"It's no secret there's no love lost between them," Noel said seriously, "but — damn it, Belinda — I just can't believe that Adam —"

Belinda gripped his hand so tight that he winced. "Noel, the *handkerchief!*"

"What handkerchief?"

"I forget to *tell* you — I found a *handkerchief* up there on the ground that night — it has an A in the corner —"

Noel looked strained. And scared. "You . . . actually have it?"

"Yes! If what we're thinking is true, if Adam dropped it up there that night — oh, God, he knows I have it —"

"How could he know?"

Belinda was babbling, tears filling up again in her eyes. "That day in his room — it fell out of my pocket — he asked me what it was."

"Do you have it now?"

"No . . . no." She shook her head miserably. "It's at home in my other jacket — but — I *know* he recognized it — he *had* to — "

"Maybe not." Noel tried to soothe her. "Maybe he didn't. And maybe we're jumping to *way* too many conclusions here —"

Noel's head snapped up, his body going stiff.

As Belinda looked on in dread, he put a finger to his lips and pried her hand from his arm.

He pointed to the door.

Trembling, Belinda nodded. She had heard it, too.

The sound in the hallway.

Slipping noiselessly across the room, Noel put his ear to the door. His hand curled around the doorknob . . . his body tensed. . . .

As the door whipped open, Belinda prepared herself for the sight of Adam and his black, accusing eyes.

Instead there was only black, empty hallway.

And the faraway sound of a door closing.

"Do you think it was him?" Belinda shuddered. "Do you think he was listening?"

"It could have been Cobbs. I heard the car pull in earlier." Noel eased the door back into place, his voice grim. "He has the most irritating habit of slipping around without making any noise when he wants to."

"But it *could* have been Adam —"

"I hope to God it wasn't. For both our sakes."

He turned back the covers and helped her into bed, tucking the blanket snugly around her chin. "Now, look. I'll push the lock on my way out. And *you* get some sleep."

"I don't like this, Noel — I don't like sleeping in the same house with Adam —"

"Nothing can happen to you in here, Belinda. And we can talk some more in the morning. I need to think about all this."

She nodded obediently, her eyes wide and frightened. As Noel looked down at her, he suddenly put a hand to her forehead and smiled.

"Don't worry, okay? I'll think of something."

For a brief moment he was framed in the doorway; the next second Belinda heard the click of the latch.

"Good night, Noel," she mumbled.

She didn't think she could sleep, but her eyes closed within minutes. Restlessly she tossed through black nightmares, pursued by blinding headlights, the deep dream-silence shattered by the blare of a horn, the growling of engines — and suddenly she was pinned beneath the merciless weight of twisted, burning wreckage . . . and invisible hands were trying to pull her out, trying to pull debris from her face and body. . . .

They were pulling something across her neck.

She could feel it — a long, thick rope — being pulled slowly and heavily across her neck . . . across her windpipe. . . .

Belinda's eyes fluttered open and she caught her breath.

The pressure on her neck was still there . . .

Still moving.

She felt its uncomfortable warmth . . . the slow, relentless tightening of its flesh . . . like one long muscle . . .

Shrieking, Belinda flung the covers back and leaped from the bed, cowering in the corner of the room as she frantically probed the slithering darkness. She was vaguely aware of feet in the hallway, of someone pounding on her door, of a voice shouting her name —

"Belinda! Belinda, are you all right? Unlock the door!"

She was terrified to cross the floor, terrified of stepping on something alive . . . deadly. . . .

"Oh, Noel!"

She threw her arms around him as he rushed into the room, and as the light came on, they stared in horror at the foot of the bed.

A four-foot-long snake was just beginning its descent onto the rug. It shrank back from the sudden glare, curling itself defensively onto the bedpost.

Through shocked eyes, Belinda saw Cobbs hesitate in the doorway, neat as a pin in bathrobe and slippers.

"You vile creature. There you are."

"What do you mean?" Noel burst out at him. "Did you know this thing was loose?"

"Since eleven o'clock tonight," Cobbs replied. "When I discovered the empty cage."

Chapter 15

Cobbs was the only one up when Belinda came down the next morning. She leaned weakly in the doorway, watching as he tied a starched white apron about himself and solemnly poured dog food into Sasha's bowl. The dog was nowhere to be seen — sleeping with Noel, Belinda guessed — but Cobbs wiped off her food mat and put fresh water in her other dish, aligning both bowls just so.

"Morning, Cobbs."

"It appears to be, miss," Cobbs responded, though he didn't turn to look at her. She plopped down at the table, surveying the room through red eyes. "Breakfast?" he asked.

"No, thanks, I couldn't," she sighed. "You didn't seem surprised to see me last night."

"Nothing in this house surprises me. Tea?"

"Thanks. Cobbs?"

"Yes, miss."

"Was Adam with you at the movies last night?"

"He was."

"Sitting right beside you the whole time? Where you could see him?"

Cobbs looked insulted. "Due to our varying tastes in films, miss, Mister Adam and I attended separate features. All in the same theater, however."

Belinda stared hard at the tabletop, her stomach suddenly queasy. "Cobbs," she said carefully, "do you think Adam's crazy?"

Cobbs cast her a disdainful look. "All teenagers are crazy. It happens to be their one constancy."

"I'm serious."

Perhaps it was her tone of voice . . . or her tear-swollen eyes . . . or merely the uncanny perception that Cobbs seemed to have. Whatever it was, Cobbs set her tea down in front of her, then took the opposite chair. His face looked rather tired.

"It happened so many years ago," he said.

"What did? You sound so mysterious." Belinda shifted nervously, and he nodded.

"It is, in a way. Because we shall probably never know."

"Know . . . what?"

"Perhaps I should start at the beginning."

"Yes. Please."

"He was a child, you understand. Only ten years of age. His parents were not on the best of terms. If was difficult for him."

"You mean they fought a lot?"

"Most unpleasant . . . most uncivil. Adam was always a quiet child . . . acutely observant . . . intense and sensitive by nature."

"Then he must have been very affected by it."

"It was, as I say, most difficult. He was immensely . . . troubled. He adored his father. Mr. Thorne, however, adored his business. Adam always came last. Or not at all."

Belinda nodded slowly, not liking the tone of his voice.

"They sent him away for a while, to some distant relatives. Adam didn't know them, and they themselves had no real love for children." He glanced at her, and she nodded again, swallowing over a lump in her throat. "There were . . . problems."

"That's so sad," Belinda murmured. "A little kid with people who didn't care about him and —" She broke off at the look on his face. "What do you mean — what kinds of problems?"

"Adam tried to run away. Several times, in fact. He claimed they were unkind to him . . . that they . . . abused him."

"Oh, no."

"They, on the other hand, insisted that he was deliberately argumentative and disobedient. They claimed he threatened them, and they wanted to send him home straightaway."

"But his parents didn't believe the aunt and uncle, did they?"

"They were involved in a bitter divorce. Adam was the furthest problem from their minds."

Belinda cradled her head on her arms, keeping her worried gaze on Cobbs. "How long did he have to stay there?"

Cobbs grew very still. "He stayed until the accident — the first one, that is."

"Adam was in . . . another accident?" Belinda felt the hair prickle along the back of her neck, and her head came up slowly.

Cobbs took a sip of tea . . . took a long time to settle the cup back in the saucer. "It was a rainy night . . . as I understand it . . . they were driving along a steep road. . . ."

Belinda strained to hear him, but suddenly his words were muffled and faraway . . . his face was blurry . . . as if nothing could quite penetrate her fear-numbed senses.

" . . . out of control," Cobbs was saying. His voice was as unemotional as his expression. "The car plunged down an embankment and caught fire. Adam's uncle was killed outright. His aunt died later that night in hospital."

"And . . ." Belinda realized she was mumbling; she didn't have the strength to make more of an effort. "And — Adam —"

"He was thrown clear. The police who found the car said it was nothing short of a miracle."

"And he wasn't hurt?" Belinda felt weak.

"He suffered a head injury." Cobbs moved at last, picked up a cloth napkin, refolded it with precise creases. "Somewhat severe. He was confined to bed for quite a long while."

"My God," Belinda murmured. *No wonder this accident has been so traumatic for him . . . it's bringing it all back again . . . all the bad memories.*

"The mood changes began soon after."

"Mood changes?"

"It was as if he was determined to isolate himself from society . . . to insulate himself from any further pain. His father, unfortunately, could not be bothered with a problem such as Adam. His mother agreed to take custody of him . . . in exchange for a substantial check the first of each month." Before Belinda could comment, he added, "She is an ineffectual woman, I fear. She has spent the last eight years of her life being afraid of the boy."

"Afraid of Adam? His own mother? But —"

"There have been frequent incidents of lying . . . often to the point of compulsiveness. His belligerence frightens her . . . he trusts no one and feels himself an outcast from others. Adam is shrewd," Cobbs looked directly into her eyes. "Like any miserable creature who's been consistently mistreated, he senses people's fears and weaknesses and uses them to his own advantage. But it was that accident that started it all."

"Started . . . what?"

"Later that night, as his aunt lay dying, she kept trying to communicate with the doctors. It was impossible to understand what she was saying, but they distinctly caught the words 'Adam' and 'steering wheel' over and over again."

"What?" Belinda gripped the edge of the table and leaned forward, her face draining white. "Cobbs, what are you saying — ?"

"The doctors said that she was highly agitated — and that until the very end she kept trying to tell them something, which they strongly felt involved Adam and the accident. Naturally, they dismissed it as a form of delirium."

Belinda pressed her hands to her head, looking up at Cobbs in dismay. "But — but you don't think it was anything *bad*, do you? She *could* have been hysterical, couldn't she, with the accident and everything? You don't *really* think Adam would — ?"

Cobbs sighed, his steady old face impassive. "Nothing was ever proved, miss. And after all . . . he was only a child."

"Why would anyone even consider it?" Belinda held her cup to her lips and realized her hands were shaking. She set it down and clenched her hands in her lap.

"Mister Adam had called home the morning of the accident. His father and mother were away, and so he spoke to me. He was crying . . ." Cobbs's voice trailed off as he looked back into his memory. His voice dropped . . . faltered. "He told . . . he told me how very unhappy he was, and that he wanted to come home. He said that if he had to stay there a single day longer . . . he would do something desperate."

There was a strange roar through her head. In her mind she saw Cobbs recede, then pull back again, and she slumped in her chair, staring at him as if she'd never seen him before. As in a dream, she saw him staring back at her, his brows drawn down over hooded eyes.

"Are you quite all right, miss?"

Her mind reeled with a whirl of impressions —
the handkerchief . . . Adam's slashed face . . . April
Fools' Day . . . the stench of the bloody doll's head
. . . the snake.

"Miss Belinda?"

"Yes." She shook her head, clearing it, and there
was a rattle of china as Cobbs took her cup for a
refill. "I . . . I don't know what to think."

Cobbs's look was matter-of-fact. "Mister Adam
is a bit of an enigma."

"He scares me," Belinda said simply. "I don't
understand him, and he scares me, Cobbs."

"He scares most people. And he intends to do
just that, I've no doubt."

"Do *you* think he caused that accident eight years
ago? Please be honest with me." She looked at him
beseechingly, and he stopped beside the table, the
sugar and creamer poised just above her cup.

"I think only Mister Adam knows the answer to
that."

Before Belinda could reply, they heard a scurry
of paws and Sasha came into the kitchen. Noel still
looked half asleep as he sat down, but he grinned
at them and brushed a stubborn shock of hair from
his forehead.

"Don't we have some good strong coffee around
here, Cobbs? I don't think this tea will get me
going."

"Perhaps you could sample my special macho
blend."

Noel grinned again, but Belinda's smile was
forced. As Sasha nudged her nose into Belinda's

hand, Noel leaned across with a frown.

"You look beat. Sleep okay?"

"Not really." She lowered her voice as Cobbs disappeared into the pantry. "Cobbs and Adam saw different movies last night. Adam could have sneaked out and —"

"Afraid not. I checked the car last night after they got in."

"You mean —"

Noel shook his head. "Not a scratch."

"Then how?" Belinda hissed. "I don't understand —"

Noel put a finger to his lips as Cobbs reappeared. "Okay, Belinda, what's your pleasure? Cobbs's culinary talents will amaze and delight you."

"I . . . uh . . ." She felt her stomach cramp just thinking of food. "I should probably get home . . . Mom'll be wondering what happened to me."

"Okay. I'll drive you." Noel pushed back from the table, and Cobbs cleared his throat.

"Mister Noel, if I might have a word —"

"Only one. Only if it's pleasant."

"It's your mother, sir."

"Forget it, Cobbs. That is *not* pleasant." Noel grinned. "Sorry. What about her?"

"She hasn't checked into her hotel. In fact, she's not expected there at all."

Noel's hand stopped halfway to Sasha's head, and he looked puzzled. "What do you mean?"

"I tried to ring her last night — with a report on Mr. Thorne. I was informed that she'd sent a facsimile message, changing her plans."

"Did she say what the change was?"

"Only that a business emergency called her away immediately."

"That's funny." Noel exchanged glances with Belinda. "Would she usually tell you when she's changing her plans?"

"It's unlikely, sir."

"Well . . ." Noel shrugged, but Belinda could see the uneasiness in his eyes. "Knowing Mom, she'll be found when she wants to be. Come on, Belinda — I'll take you home."

"Wait — I forgot my purse. Thanks for everything, Cobbs. Noel, I'll meet you outside, okay?"

It only took a few minutes to retrieve her purse from the bedroom. As Belinda caught a glimpse of gray sky past the window, she shivered and zipped up her jacket, suddenly remembering the handkerchief. *I've got to remember to show it to Noel when I get home. . . .* For a moment she stood beside the bed, remembering his kiss, the way he'd held her. The gown lay folded on the bed now, and she looked at it wistfully. And then she remembered her nightmare — that feeling of suffocating — waking up with the snake across her neck —

Another chill went through her, and she hurried back down the hall, slowing a little as she spotted a half-open door and a dim glow slanting across the corridor. She stopped and stared at it, wondering if someone had accidentally left a light on that she should turn off. But as she started in, there came a faint sound of drawers opening and shutting, the soft rustle of papers.

Cautiously . . . slowly . . . Belinda peeked around the door, squinting against the narrow glare of a lamp that angled down onto a desk.

What she could see of the room appeared to be an office, or a study.

And then she saw him.

Adam was bent over the desk, one hand grasping the edge of a drawer, the other holding a thick sheaf of papers. As his lips moved silently, he seemed to be mouthing whatever he was reading, his head shaking slowly from side to side. And then, as she watched curiously, his eyes narrowed, the hand on the drawer moving slowly up to clutch the other side of the papers. In the eerie half-light, he looked like he was smiling.

He lowered the pages.

And then he let them go, sheet after sheet fluttering like fragile wings to the desktop.

He gathered them up. And thrust them in a drawer. And locked it.

Belinda saw him hide the key inside a book on a paneled shelf.

In the shadows his eyes glittered with a strange light.

And he began to laugh . . . deeply . . . horribly.

It was a cruel sound, without feeling.

And as Belinda turned and ran, she realized that Adam's laugh hadn't even sounded human.

Chapter 16

"Something in the desk," Belinda said again. "He was laughing . . . he sounded horrible —"

"But what was he doing in Fred's study? Did he see you?" Noel glanced at her anxiously as he turned onto her street. "Did he know you were there?"

"No, I'm sure he didn't." Belinda gazed unhappily out at her old, familiar neighborhood. "But what do you think it means?"

"I don't know, but I'm sure going to find out."

"Noel . . . I've been thinking —" Belinda faced him, all seriousness. "Maybe we shouldn't see each other anymore."

The car nearly went onto the sidewalk as Noel stared at her. Quickly he got it under control, but his voice was astonished as he gave her a teasing grin. "Only one date and I get the brush-off? *One* date? *Two* kisses and *one* date?"

In spite of herself Belinda chuckled. "It doesn't have anything to do with you —"

"Oh, right. You don't want to see me again, but

it's not personal." His eyes twinkled, warming her. "Okay, what's wrong now?"

"It's just that . . . well, after what happened last night, if Adam *is* after me, then you nearly got killed because you were with me."

"I can't think of a nicer way to go —"

"Noel, I'm serious! Please — I don't want you to get hurt —"

"And I don't want *you* to get hurt. Will you be okay at home today? Till I get back later?"

"Yes, but —"

"Look." He reached over and found her hand, his fingers entwining with hers. "Until we're sure what's going on here, I'm afraid you're stuck with me. End of discussion. Now shape up — there's your mom."

Mrs. Swanson was just pulling into the driveway as they drove up. Belinda introduced her to Noel who politely declined an offer for coffee, saying he'd promised an emergency run to the grocery store for Cobbs and needed to get back. Belinda watched him drive away, and as she turned back toward the house, Mom gave an approving nod.

"He's cute."

"Yes." Belinda nodded with her, smiling. "And very sweet."

"And charming to mothers. The young man knows how to make points. So how are *you* feeling? I *knew* you'd come down with something sooner or later — the way you've been working so hard —"

"Whoa. I'm much, much better."

"Hmmm . . . now, would *that* have anything to do with Noel?"

They laughed and went inside, and though Mrs. Swanson was dead on her feet, she insisted on hearing all about the picnic before she went to bed. Belinda fixed coffee, trying to recall funny incidents she knew her mother would enjoy . . . friends her mother would recognize . . . anything but the terror that had followed them on into the night.

"I'm glad you had such a good time, honey." Mom leaned back, looking truly pleased. "And I'm glad Noel's such a nice boy. Think you'll be seeing much of each other?"

"I don't know how long he's staying in town," Belinda said evasively. "*And* — in case you haven't noticed — our worlds are *very* different." She gave a wry smile, looking up as Mom's hand covered her own.

"I didn't notice that it bothered him. And if it doesn't bother *him*, there's no reason at all why it should bother you."

Belinda nodded, remembering last night, Noel's kisses, hoping her flushed cheeks wouldn't give her away.

"And anyway" — Mom patted her and stifled a yawn — "you make a very attractive couple."

"You'd say that about anyone I went out with," Belinda scolded.

"Wrong. I didn't say that about Homer Washburn."

"Homer Washburn picked his nose, and we were only in the third grade!"

"See? I rest my case." Mom blew her a kiss from the doorway. "See you later, sweetie pie — these double shifts can't last forever."

" 'Bye, Mom," Belinda said fondly, blowing her a kiss back. She watched the empty threshold with a queer, aching loneliness, wishing for the hundredth time that things — *everything* — could be normal again.

The phone rang, and Belinda scrambled to answer it, brightening when she heard Hildy's voice.

"Where on earth have you been? Don't lie to me, Belinda Swanson, I know you didn't come home last night — I called *forever!*"

"There was an . . . emergency." Belinda smiled, imagining Hildy's expression all too clearly. "I had to spend the night at Noel's."

"Did you say *at* Noel's . . . or *with* Noel?" Hildy's voice lowered. "I have to hear all the details —"

"I'm afraid you won't really want to. They're not what you expect."

"What's that supposed to mean?"

"Can you meet me? The mall in half an hour?"

"I'll be there."

Belinda left a note against the coffeepot, grabbed an umbrella, then took off on foot down the street. Rain came down in a soft, steady drizzle, and the world lay drenched around her, soggy and cold. There weren't many people out today — even the traffic seemed lighter than usual for a Saturday. Walking slowly along, Belinda tried to remember how she had felt a month ago, before everything had happened. . . . She closed her eyes against the stinging chill, then opened them, not sure if her sudden tears were from the wind or her own despair.

And suddenly she wasn't on the sidewalk anymore, beneath the spreading trees of a quiet, old neighborhood . . . she was back on that hillside and it was April Fools' Day and while someone screamed in agony from a burning car, a figure stood on the crest of the hill . . . not helping . . . not answering . . . just watching.

And again she could see Hildy and Frank, coming so slowly . . . and all the while shouting her name . . . shouting at the tops of their lungs . . . *"Belinda! Belinda!"*

With a sudden, inexplicable feeling of dread, Belinda cast a look over her shoulder and began to run.

She ran through puddles — she slipped and fell — she scrambled up again and ran on —

Run, Belinda Swanson . . . run for your life.

As the mall appeared at last, she raced into its noisy, crowded corridors. Hildy was waiting at their usual meeting place, and when Belinda collapsed into the chair beside her, Hildy jumped up in alarm.

"My God, what happened to you?"

"Nothing. I . . . nothing."

"You act like someone's after you. Is someone after you?" Hildy scanned the crowds nervously, but Belinda pulled her back down.

"Sit down and listen to me. I'm not imagining things this time. We're all in real danger —"

"What are you *talking* about?"

"Listen — *please* — just be quiet and *listen!* What if we really *didn't* have anything to do with Adam's accident —"

"Oh, for God's sake, Belinda, that's what we've been trying to tell you —"

"Shut up, Hildy! Please! Look" — Belinda clamped down on her friend's arm — "what if the *driver* caused the accident, but we were there and he jumped out and saw us and heard you calling my name —"

"Wait — stop — you are not making *any* sense at all —"

"Yes! Yes, I am — just listen — think back to that night, okay? Okay? The man. The man on the hill —"

"Belinda, what *man?* You're the only one who saw someone there, and Frank and I still think —"

"What if it was Adam?"

Hildy's eyes narrowed, fastened on Belinda's face . . . widened again as she drew back.

"What if the person I saw on the hill was Adam. What if Adam caused the wreck, and somehow escaped and he saw us there. And now he's chasing me because I have his handkerchief and he doesn't want any witnesses —"

"What handkerchief? Is this some joke you and Frank are — ?"

"I'm *serious*, damn it! What if Adam's trying to *kill* me!"

Hildy stared at her for a long moment. She chewed thoughtfully on the end of one silver braid . . . shook her head slowly. She saw the desperation in Belinda's eyes . . . then the blazing anger as Belinda pulled a handkerchief out of her pocket and shook it under Hildy's nose.

"That is *disgusting!*" Hildy made a face. "What are you carrying that disgusting thing around for anyway — ?"

Belinda cut her off sharply. "I found it. That night. Remember when I fell in front of Frank's car and my nose started bleeding —"

"Well . . . not really . . . sort of, I guess —"

"This was on the ground, and I picked it up and used it. See the bloodstains —"

"I *see* them, Belinda." Hildy grimaced. "Get that thing *away* from me."

"Okay, now, just listen — Hildy, *please* — you've got to see how this is all fitting together —"

"What I'm *seeing* is you going insane right in front of my eyes." Hildy pulled back with an exasperated sigh. "But, go ahead, I'm listening."

"When I was with Adam the other day he saw this handkerchief — he asked where I got it."

"So what."

"Don't you see? He *saw* that I had the handkerchief. If he saw that I had it, then he's positive I was there at the crash."

Hildy considered a moment. "Why are you so sure it's his?"

"Look here — the initial?"

"Belinda!" Hildy gaped at her. "It could be *anybody's* handkerchief! You can buy these at any store anywhere in the country! For crying out loud, look at this old thing. You don't know how long it could have been lying out there — it could have been there for months and months." She gave a shudder. "Ugh. I just hope you didn't catch some disease from it or something."

"Someone followed Noel and me last night — we could have been killed — someone tried to run us off the road!"

"Are you . . . serious?"

Belinda's fingers cut into her wrist. "Adam was in an accident when he was ten years old — his aunt and uncle died, but Adam didn't — don't you understand? That accident he had before sounds *exactly* like the accident he was just in — *the one we saw!*"

Hildy was staring at her in shocked silence. Belinda shook her by the shoulders.

"You see, don't you? How it all makes sense?"

"Nothing's making sense. Least of all, *you.*"

"Oh, God." Belinda's eyes lowered to her hands, to her fingers working nervously in the folds of the handkerchief. "Don't you see that he really could be . . . completely crazy?"

"*You're* crazy, Belinda. Forget about Adam. You're the one who's completely crazy. Totally over the edge."

"I'm not," Belinda said tightly. "I'm not —"

"Okay, then, *if* Adam's some kind of murderer, then how does he get around? Fly? And how come he wants to kill his father in the first place? Motive, Detective Swanson!"

"Maybe he doesn't need a motive. When you're

crazy, you don't need a motive, you just do it because you're crazy —"

"Stop. I don't want to hear any more of this. Ever since this thing started, Frank and I have worried about you — you took it all way too seriously. And now look. You've woven this whole *fantasy* around this stupid April Fools' joke, and you've talked yourself into believing it was the *same* accident and that it was our fault." She paused, but Belinda wouldn't look up. "I thought you'd snap out of it. I thought, with a little time, you'd lighten up and see how it didn't matter! But now you've gone and concocted this whole new horror story about Adam being crazy and Adam being a murderer. God, poor *Adam*, does he even realize how screwed up he is there inside *your* head?" Hildy stared at her, pleading. "Belinda — please — *please* stop all this. You've always been so level-headed and calm about things — and now you're just . . . you're just . . ."

"Someone tried to kill me last night, Hildy. Do you think I imagined that? Do you think Noel imagined it? Do you want to see his car?" Belinda's voice shook dangerously. "Even *Noel* thinks I have a reason to be scared about all this —"

She broke off, shocked, as Hildy began to cry —

"Did you *tell* Noel? *Did* you? You *promised* — we made a *pact* —" She backed away from Belinda, her eyes hard and accusing as she sobbed angrily. "I *told* Frank not to do it! I *told* him not to, but he said it'd be *funny*! He said it was just a *joke*, and he promised he'd tell you about it later —"

"What?" Belinda's words came out slowly, be-

tween clenched teeth. "What — are — you — talking — about?"

Hildy wrapped her arms around her chest, as if
to shield herself from the slow dawn of realization
in Belinda's eyes. "The package on your porch —
that calendar — *Frank* did that. And the day those
police came to your house —"

Belinda's body went numb; her eyes burned with
hurt and rage. "And that night — in the parking
lot — the voice at my window — I bet you two
really had a good laugh about that."

Hildy was crying harder now, and several people
had stopped to stare. "I don't know anything about
that — I didn't have anything to do with those —"

"Oh, Hildy, *stop* it! How long did you two plan?
Scare Belinda to death — what fun! Call Belinda a
murderer — April Fools', huh?"

"I swear, Belinda, I *swear!* I don't know anything
about those things — if Frank did them, I didn't
know! I wouldn't have done that to you, I swear I
wouldn't —"

"Oh, right." Belinda was striding through the
mall now, elbowing her way through packs of shop-
pers. She could hear Hildy racing behind her, begging her to stop, but all she could see were the exit
doors and the gray world beyond, and all she could
think about was getting to Frank —

"Belinda, *please!*" Hildy grabbed her from behind, and Belinda swung to face her. Belinda was
so furious that she spat out her words.

"Where's Frank now?"

"Don't go over there — don't tell him I told

you — it's not worth it, Belinda, it was just a *joke* —" She whimpered as Belinda grabbed her and shook her hard.

"Where *is* he?"

"I — I don't know — the gym pool, he's practicing at the pool — we didn't mean it, Belinda — you've got to *believe* that — we'd never have hurt you —"

Belinda burst through the doors, leaving Hildy crying in the middle of the corridor. She realized she'd left her umbrella, but she didn't care — she welcomed the rain falling all around her, heavier now than it had been before, closing her in from the rest of the world. She raced deliberately through puddles, soaking her feet and clothes, and with every dogged step her mind laughed at her. *Friends*, it said, and as she went faster it laughed even more — *friends — friends — friends —*

"I don't have any friends," Belinda told herself angrily, and she wiped at her face, wiping away rain — only rain — and not a single tear. She could hear Hildy running behind her, trying to keep up, but she didn't slow down, and she wouldn't stop.

The school was a good distance away, but Belinda wanted to go on foot — she relished the determination building up inside her with every block, the hate and anger and the painful scorch of betrayal — they felt good somehow, and justified, and she fed them with memories of all that she and Hildy and Frank had shared, and they dug deeper and hurt even more. She was surprised when she saw the gym in front of her, a bleak shadow through the rain — she couldn't remember having gotten there, and as she tugged open the doors she seemed to be standing off watching herself.

"Frank."

It wasn't a call exactly, certainly not a question. The room was dark, but she saw the lights on in the pool and knew without a doubt that he was there. She walked closer, her heart like a rock in the pit of her stomach, her hands clenched and trembling at her sides.

"I know you're here, Frank. Come on out."

And yet, somewhere far in the back of her mind she thought it was strange that he didn't answer . . . that some snide remark didn't stop her at the edge of the pool . . . that some hurtful joke didn't challenge her as she searched through the dim light for his leering face.

"Come on out, King of Fools — the joke's over."

And she waited for his laugh to echo from the tiled walls . . . to ripple across the quiet, shadowy water. . . .

It *was* shadowy, she realized uneasily. Standing at the water's edge, she saw murky shapes oozing across the uneasy surface . . . playing sly tricks with her eyes . . . luring them to the far end where a deep, deep shadow lay, and lay so very still. . . .

One deep shadow . . .

Deeper and blacker than the rest . . .

Shapeless and bobbing in the cloudy, dark water . . .

"Frank!"

She felt an icy shock as she dived in — heard her

own quick gasp of horror and the faraway panic of Hildy's scream. . . .

And then the world went silent. . . .

Frank . . .

Silent as a tomb, far, far, from the living.

Oh, God . . . Frank . . .

Silent as the thing that floated and twisted limply in her arms.

Chapter 17

"Stop it, Hildy — *stop it!*"

Belinda pulled herself weakly to the side of the pool, Hildy's hysterical sobs echoing over and over, strangely hollow in the huge, shadowy emptiness. Belinda lay her head down on the cool, rough surface, but her body was trembling so violently she could hardly hold herself up out of the water.

"Stop it, Hildy! It's not Frank. It's only his jacket."

The crying checked itself . . . gurgled down to a low moan. Belinda peered up at her with blazing eyes.

"You planned this, too, didn't you? That I'd come over here looking for him? Very convincing — maybe you should take up acting —"

"Screw you, Belinda!" Hildy's foot stomped, missing Belinda's hand by inches, causing her to jerk back in surprise. "Screw you! Do I look like I'm *acting?*"

Belinda stared at her, studying the crumpled face, the long streaks of ruined makeup, the quivering chin. "Well, what do you expect me to think after what you — ?"

"I thought that was *him!*" Hildy cried. "I thought Frank was *dead* —"

"Ssh, Hildy, okay, okay — don't fall apart on me —"

"But I bet you're disappointed, aren't you, Belinda? That Frank's *not* dead? Come on, admit it — just 'cause you can't take a joke —"

"Come on, Hildy, you know better than that —"

"Is it 'cause you're still jealous?" Hildy's voice was getting louder, ricocheting off the walls, slapping at Belinda's pride. "Just because Frank loves *me* and not *you?*"

In spite of her numbness, Belinda felt anger surge through her, her cheeks burning hot. "It has nothing to do with that."

"Right, I really believe you! You're just *jealous!* Because Frank picked *me!* He told me how you threw yourself at him and —"

"I *never* threw myself at him!" Belinda burst out indignantly. "Don't you see this is just another trick of his — to make himself look wonderful?"

"He *is* wonderful!" Hildy was crying again, her face livid. "He's handsome — he's popular — he has a great sense of humor —"

"A *great* sense of humor," Belinda echoed bitterly. "I can see how much he made you laugh just now —" She threw Frank's wet jacket at Hildy's feet. "Very entertaining."

In the flickering shadows, Hildy's cat-eyes glistened, filled with hate. "I'd like to hurt you, Belinda — really hurt you."

Stunned, Belinda stared back, her heart hammering in her throat, choking back sudden tears. "Oh, Hildy . . . you don't really mean that —"

In answer, Hildy spun around and started for the door. She almost had it open when Belinda's voice stopped her.

"Wait — Hildy — please. Let's not fight like this, we've been friends too long. Just listen to me —" Belinda hoisted herself up out of the pool, collapsing onto the side in a soggy heap. "This jacket — if Frank *wasn't* trying to play a joke on me — or us — then . . . what if something really happened to him? What if he really *was* here — practicing, like you said — and the person who's been after me found him and —"

Hildy stiffened, but she didn't turn around. "You just don't give up, do you?" Furiously she swung open the door, crashing it back against the wall. "I'm going to Frank's right now, and we're going to have a *wonderful* weekend together — without you." And as Belinda stared openmouthed, Hildy paused in the doorway, her head a silvery silhouette. "We're not friends anymore."

"Hildy!" Belinda scrambled up, pushing back her wet hair with trembling fingers. "It *could* happen — to *any* of us — I could be next — or you —"

"I don't want to be your friend, Belinda," Hildy said quietly.

Before she even realized what she was doing,

Belinda picked up the wad of jacket and flung it as hard as she could, splattering Hildy from head to toe. "And since when were you *ever* my friend, Hildy? Since *when?*"

The door closed, leaving Belinda in thick silence. Across the tiles, shadows rippled like hundreds of restless snakes, and the lights in the pool dimmed and flickered beneath the water. She covered her face with her hands, too exhausted to cry, and then slowly she started for home.

Mrs. Swanson was at the kitchen table reading a magazine when Belinda dragged through the door. She surveyed her bedraggled daughter in surprise, then looked out the window at the rainy afternoon.

"You must've gotten caught in a downpour! Why didn't you take an umbrella?"

"I left it at the mall." Belinda paused beside the counter, hanging her head, trying not to cry. She thought of Cobbs and how good his tea would taste right about now. . . .

"Belinda?"

She jumped as her mother came up beside her and laid a cool hand across her forehead.

"I'm okay, Mom."

"Get out of those wet things before you catch cold."

"I'm really okay."

"Hmmm . . . I'm not so sure." She waited until Belinda reappeared in her robe, then wrapped her daughter's fingers around a mug of coffee as they sat down at the table.

"Belinda?" Her mother waited, studying the drawn look on Belinda's face.

"Well . . . Hildy and I sort of had a fight."

"Why did I figure something like that?" Mrs. Swanson gave a knowing smile. "Look, honey . . . I don't know what went on between you two, and it's none of my business unless you want it to be. But it's very normal for people to say things they don't really mean when they're upset. You and Hildy have been friends for a long time. I hope you can look past the hurt and be patient. She *will* realize — eventually — how much your friendship means."

Belinda felt an ironic smile forming on her lips. *Friendship.* She'd come to know quite a lot about Hildy's idea of friendship lately. *Oh, Mom, if you only knew. . . .*

"Better?" Mrs. Swanson pressed her thumbs against Belinda's forehead, a firm yet gentle pressure as she smoothed the worry lines away. "I'm going to call the hospital and take a couple extra hours off — and *you're* going to lie down. And then, after you've rested, I'll beat your socks off at Scrabble, what do you say?"

"I say you're dreaming."

"Get out of here."

Smiling, Belinda went to her room and stretched out across her bed. She closed her eyes and tried to empty her mind, but all she could think about was what Hildy had said at the pool . . . the look of fury on her face . . . the confession she'd made at the mall . . . Frank's jacket floating . . . floating. . . .

And then, like a bad dream, she remembered telling her whole awful story last night . . . and how there had been that noise in the hallway . . . like somebody listening . . . only nobody had been there. . . .

"Hildy," Belinda mumbled drowsily. *I'm tired of looking out for you anyway . . . you're on your own, and that's fine with me.*

She plunged into sleep and tossed on half-formed dreams. She heard the rain streaming into her unconscious . . . and it became a muffled underwater roar . . . and suddenly she was Frank, sinking lifelessly to the bottom of a deep, dark pool.

"Frank!"

She sat up with a start. Her door was closed and the room was pitch dark. She felt stiff and sore . . . surprised to find a blanket over her. Mom must have come in and covered her up . . . how long had she been asleep?

The chime of the doorbell echoed down the hallway. She heard voices in the living room, and when a tap sounded on the bedroom door, she remembered that Noel was coming by. A moment later he stood self-consciously in the doorway, while Belinda blinked against the light.

"Hi — uh . . . your mom said to come on back, but I can wait out here —"

"No, come in. Just don't look at me, I'm a mess." She made a face at herself in the mirror as Noel sat down on the edge of the bed.

"Are you okay?" His voice sounded tight . . . worried. "I mean, your mom's still here. . . ." He trailed off, studying her with anxious eyes.

"She's just going to work a little late today — in fact, she's probably leaving any minute." Belinda winced as she tried to brush the tangles from her hair. "Guess I slept too long to beat her at Scrabble."

"She said you've been asleep for hours."

"I guess I was. Not that I slept all that great." She paused, her brush in midair. "I had this nightmare about Frank. That something awful had happened to him . . . that he was dead."

Noel looked startled. "Dead?"

"But I know where it came from." Belinda sighed. "This afternoon I found Frank's jacket floating in the swimming pool where he always practices — it looked like a dead body. I thought he was just playing another joke, but . . . I don't know." She took an angry swipe at her hair. "Hildy and I had a fight afterward and she went off in a huff to find Frank, and I was mad at both of them. I — Noel?"

His eyes lifted guiltily, meeting her reflection. "I'm sorry, Belinda — what?"

"Are you listening to a thing I've said?"

"I'm sorry . . . it's my stepfather." Noel looked uncomfortable as Belinda turned to face him. "The hospital called this evening . . . they don't think he'll live through the night. I . . . kind of feel like I should be there."

"Oh, Noel, I'm so sorry." Belinda shut her eyes,

forcing away the images of death that kept crowding in. "Does Adam know?"

"Cobbs said he'd tell him after I left just now. I'm . . . not very good at that sort of thing. Not that Adam will be especially upset," he added grimly.

Belinda remembered the phone conversation she'd overheard. ". . . *the waiting . . . we've waited long enough.*" She shivered and reached out for his arm. "And what about your mother?"

"I just can't figure it out." Noel shook his head. "I still haven't heard from her. You'd think with Fred so bad, she'd at least —"

"You . . . don't think something's happened to her?" Belinda said suddenly. She felt him stiffen. The look he gave her was uneasy.

"But wouldn't we have heard something? I mean, if something's wrong, you'd think we'd hear something, wouldn't you?"

"I'm sure nothing's wrong," Belinda said quickly. "I don't know why I said that."

"I do. You were thinking about Adam again. About the talk you and I had last night." Noel rose slowly from the bed and took her into his arms. "But Adam couldn't have done anything to Mom — Adam's been here the whole time she's been gone."

"I know. I know you're right. So what do you think we should do? Go to the police?"

"And tell them what? My mother's suddenly missing? And I just happen to have an evil stepbrother?" His mouth moved in a half smile. "We don't have any kind of proof, Belinda; there's nothing to tell the police."

She clung to him for a moment, and then as she heard footsteps in the hall, she reluctantly pulled away.

"That's Mom — I'd better tell her good-bye."

"And I'd better get home, find out what's going on."

"Oh — do you think you could just give me a ride on the way?"

"Sure." Noel smiled. "A secret rendezvous right behind my back?"

Belinda smoothed the stubborn blonde hair off his forehead. "Hardly. I just want to see Hildy, that's all."

"But I thought —"

"I know, I know, but really, I can't stand for things to be like this. We've been friends too long, and we need to get it straightened out." Her voice trembled; she brought it under control. "It really hurts me."

"Okay," Noel said softly. He looked down at her, at her worried face, and then he pulled her against his chest. "I wish nothing could ever hurt you, Belinda. I wish that more than anything."

She wanted to stay that way forever — pressed close to him, his face buried in her hair. When they finally broke apart, Noel lifted her chin and smiled into her eyes.

"I guess I owe Hildy a lot. After all, she picked you out for me."

Belinda managed a laugh. "She said one day I'd thank her for it."

"No, *I'm* the one who should thank her for it."

Noel went outside while Belinda changed, and when she came into the kitchen a few minutes later her mother was hurrying out the back door with a cheery wave.

"See you later, honey — I'm leaving you in good hands."

" 'Bye, Mom." Belinda flushed, catching Noel's amused glance. "Noel's going to take me to Hildy's —"

"I'm glad, honey!" She yelled from the car as she backed it down the drive and onto the street. "Don't worry — I'm sure it'll all work out!"

"I hope so." Belinda locked the door and followed Noel to the car, flashing him a grateful smile. "I really appreciate this — I know you're in a hurry."

"Not especially. It's not something I'm looking forward to." Noel slid in beside her and started the engine. "Okay, how do I get to Hildy's?"

"It's not far — just six blocks over. You can just drop me off."

"And what if she's not there? I'd better wait and make sure."

"Don't be silly, I can walk back."

"Don't *you* be silly, it's almost dark and — now what's this?"

Belinda turned to see a car blocking them in the drive. A man was heading for the door so she got out to intercept him.

"Oh, hi, didn't see you there." The man put a

finger to his cap and squinted down at the manila envelope in his hand. "Something for Miss . . . Swanson."

"I'll take it," Belinda said.

"Fine with me."

"Wait — where's this from?"

"You got me, lady. Some guy handed it to me — gave me ten bucks to deliver it."

"Some guy?"

"Yeah. I would've had it here a lot sooner, but I couldn't find the street."

The man took off, and Noel came around to her side of the car, looking puzzled.

"That's kind of weird, isn't it? We should have asked what the other guy looked like."

Belinda spun around, but the stranger's car was just rounding the corner. "Noel . . ." She was staring at the envelope apprehensively, and he studied the handwriting on the front.

"Let me see that."

"I don't like this. It doesn't seem right —"

"Don't open it." He pried her fingers gently from the packet and frowned down at the thing in his hand. "Is it for your mom?"

"It says *Ms.* Swanson — oh, Noel, I'm afraid to open this —"

"Here." He slid his finger beneath the flap of the envelope . . . looked cautiously inside. His frown deepened.

"Noel . . . what is it . . . what's wrong?"

She saw him turn the envelope upside down and give it an impatient shake into the palm of his hand.

She saw the envelope flutter to the pavement . . . and the long, coiled, silvery thing dangling from Noel's fingers. . . .

"What the hell — ?" As Noel looked at her in dismay, Belinda choked back a scream. "It looks like — "

"Hair," Belinda whispered. "Oh, God . . . it's one of Hildy's braids."

Chapter 18

"We have to *do* something! We have to call the police!"

"And tell them what? You don't even know if it's hers." Noel's voice struggled for calm, but he looked shaken.

"Of *course* it's hers. No one else in the world has hair like that. Oh, God — what are we going to do? We have to find her right away!"

But when they got to Hildy's house, the place was dark and no one answered the bell. A quick drive to Frank's wasn't any more successful — trying her best to appear normal, Belinda was informed by Frank's father that neither Frank nor Hildy had been there since early that morning. Back in the car again, Belinda collapsed in tears.

"You don't *know* that's Hildy's hair." Noel's face was set and pensive. "You don't *know* that anything's happened to her. She could be anywhere . . . doing anything."

"She was too *upset* to go anywhere! The only place she would have gone was to Frank's."

"Well, they're probably just off somewhere together."

"You don't really believe that, do you? Don't you see what's happening — I *knew* someone was listening at the door last night! He heard everything we said —"

"Belinda, Adam was home when I left just now. He couldn't have —"

"Then what's happening, Noel? It's something really terrible, I can feel it —"

"Okay . . . okay . . . calm down." Noel held up his hands, started the car. "We'll go back to my place, and you can stay with Cobbs."

"I don't want to go to your house! I want to find Hildy!"

"You can use the phone there and call around town, call your friends, the places she might hang out. I'm telling you, she and Frank probably just *went* somewhere — " Noel's face wore a helpless look, and Belinda shook her head fiercely.

"But you just said Adam's there."

"Then you'll see for yourself he can't be with Hildy." Noel glanced over, his voice pleading. "Look, Belinda . . . if you can't find Hildy by the time I get back, then we'll call the police, okay?"

She hesitated . . . finally nodded. Noel looked so strained . . . he had so much on his mind, and he was trying so hard to reassure her. Guiltily she thought of Hildy, so angry with her at the pool . . . she thought of Hildy's threat — *"I'd like to hurt you, Belinda . . . really hurt you."*

"Noel," Belinda said slowly, "do you think Hildy

could be playing a trick on me?" And she told him
about Hildy's outburst that afternoon. When she
finished the story, Noel's lips were pressed into an
angry line.

"I'm sorry, Belinda," he said tightly. "I'm sorry
you're so scared about Hildy, but I'd sure like to
know what kind of friend would talk that way, much
less think it was funny."

They didn't speak again all the way to the house.
Belinda's heart felt heavy as she followed Noel to
the kitchen, as she sat down on the floor and gave
Sasha a long, hard hug. Cobbs was nowhere to be
seen, and as Belinda went over to the phone, she
saw a notepad propped on the counter.

SITUATION CRITICAL. GONE TO HOSPITAL.

Her hand faltered as she picked it up and gave
it to Noel. "It's your stepfather. You'd better go."

He stared at the message for a moment, his face
weary. "It's really true then. I guess I never really
thought . . ." He turned away and Belinda came up
behind him, putting a hand on his shoulder.

"I'm so sorry. . . ."

"I didn't know him that well," Noel said softly.
"Probably no better than Adam did. He's just someone . . . you know . . . my mom lived with. Still
. . . he was a really generous guy . . . I guess he
made her happy."

Belinda wondered how it would feel to be dying,
to know that there was really no one in the world
who cared about you. To have a son and a stepson

who were practically strangers . . . a wife who was only interested in the money. It made her sad, thinking of his aloneness . . . and, as if reading her mind, Noel said, "At least he has Cobbs."

"Yes." Belinda smiled. "Good old Cobbs. I imagine he's come to the rescue on more than one occasion —" The phone rang shrilly, and she jumped. Noel answered it cautiously.

"Hello?"

Belinda watched him for several minutes. She could hear the abruptness of someone on the other end, and after nodding, Noel mumbled, "Okay, I'll be there," and slowly replaced the receiver. "Adam's at the hospital," he said. "He thinks I'd better come."

Belinda put a hand to his cheek, not knowing what to say, and he nodded at the phone. "You'd better keep calling Hildy," he reminded her gently. "Adam will be with me — you'll be safe here."

She swallowed hard. Nodded.

"I'll try to see if I can find out anything . . . if Adam —" Noel left the thought unfinished. "Will you be okay?"

Heart sinking, she forced a smile. "Of course I will."

"Keep everything locked. Don't open the door to anyone. Not anyone."

She nodded mechanically, forcing down the lump in her throat. "I'll be fine. I hope . . . you're okay."

"Thanks." He pulled her close and his lips met hers. Belinda felt frightened as he pulled away. "See you later. I'll call as soon as I can."

"Please hurry —" Belinda felt ashamed as she said it, ashamed that she could even consider needing his attention as his stepfather lay dying. "And, Noel . . . be careful."

"I will."

She heard the front door close as she picked up the phone and dialed Hildy's number. There was no answer, so she counted to ten and dialed again. Still no answer. *Where are you, Hildy? Trying to scare me . . . get back at me? Or trapped somewhere, praying for me to find you.* For one wild minute she actually considered going out to look for her, but she stopped herself at the door. No, she'd promised Noel she'd stay in and keep the doors locked. *Oh, Hildy, are you all right?*

It was such a sick thing to do . . . something Frank would do and find hysterically funny. She thought of his jacket, floating lifelessly in the dark depths of the pool. She saw Hildy's accusing eyes . . . heard the tone of her voice . . . *"not friends anymore. . . ."*

She picked up the phone and dialed again. The phone rang and rang. She paced nervously around the kitchen, Sasha watching her with good-natured interest. Again Belinda dialed the phone. Again there was nothing. Sasha's tail thumped consolingly against the floor.

And then Sasha growled.

Belinda froze, her eyes following Sasha's stare into the hall. The dog's body was tensed, the warning bubbling up from deep in her chest.

"What is it, girl? Good Sasha — show me."

The dog rose slowly, each muscle in turn. There was a long stripe of raised fur down her back, and Belinda was suddenly afraid to follow her. Sasha lowered her head and crept up the stairs, then stopped, tail quivering. Belinda's mind reeled, trying to remember which rooms lay in that direction — bedrooms . . . bathrooms . . . Mr. Thorne's study. . . .

Sasha sank slowly down onto her stomach, whining softly.

Belinda forced herself to go down the hall.

The thick carpet muffled her footsteps and she had an eerie sensation of floating. As she came up behind Sasha, the dog shifted nervously and looked at the study door. It was halfway open and the room lay dark and silent beyond.

Heart hammering, Belinda put a cautious hand to the door. It squeaked back, ten times louder in the quiet. Sasha pulled to her feet, head down, and Belinda slid her hand around the wall, searching for a light switch. She didn't even realize she'd been holding her breath until the light flicked on and she let out a sigh.

The room was empty; the desk still littered with papers. Belinda ran one hand along the polished oak, a frown creasing her brow. When had she been in here last — yesterday? The day before? With everything that had happened, it was hard to remember details of the last few weeks — only that they ran together in confused muddles, full of fear. But yes, now she remembered. It had been yesterday, and Adam had been in here.

She circled the desk slowly, still hearing his awful laugh. Her eyes dropped . . . saw the top middle drawer . . . the bundle of papers squeezing out, as if someone had thrust them away in a great hurry.

He put the papers in a drawer and hid the key in a book.

Turning around, she stared helplessly at the paneled walls, the thick bindings lining the shelves. She couldn't recall the exact spot . . . *somewhere around here* . . . and as she pulled out volume after cumbersome volume, an insistence grew inside her, pressing her on — *here . . . somewhere . . . I've got to find it.*

She tugged hard on a book and heard the key hit the floor at her feet.

Sasha glanced nervously at the empty doorway and whined.

Sliding the key into the lock, Belinda tugged at the drawer.

It held fast.

She tugged at it again, and it sprang open, papers spilling out into her hand. She could tell at first glance that they were official — the red stamped "DRAFT" across the top of several — but the pages were out of order. As she riffled through them, bits and pieces of words and phrases leaped out at her, burning into her brain — things that caused her hands to start shaking.

. . . make, publish, and declare this my Last Will and Testament, and revoke all prior Wills and Codicils that I have made. . . .

If my spouse does not survive me . . . then I

*give and bequeath all of the property described
. . . to my child and stepchild who survive me in
substantially equal shares . . . when each such child
shall attain the age of eighteen (18) years. . . .*

And then she found the one sheet that confirmed
it all.

*Last Will and Testament of Frederick Adam
Thorne.*

"Adam," Belinda murmured.

And suddenly it was all too clear . . . so shockingly
and horribly clear . . . the accident . . . and Mr.
Thorne dying . . . and she and Noel being merci-
lessly . . . relentlessly run off the road. . . .

It was you, Adam. I was right all along.

And Cobbs relating that story in the kitchen.
*". . . until the very end she kept trying to tell them
something . . . involved Adam and the accident
. . . he said . . . he would do something desperate. . . ."*

Mrs. Thorne had mysteriously disappeared.

Mr. Thorne would not live through the night.

So now that left Noel.

Noel, who would come into half the inheritance.

Noel, who stood in the way of what Adam
wanted.

Noel. Who had been lured away by a phone call
from Adam.

"Noel . . ." Belinda shut her eyes, a cry struggling
up from her throat . . . "Oh, God —"

Adam had been watching from the hill that night.

And she had picked up his handkerchief.

And he couldn't afford any witnesses . . . any evidence.

The phone blared, and she screamed, jumping back, the papers scattering over the floor.

It rang . . . and it rang . . . and she stared with wide eyes —

"I'll call you as soon as I can."

"Noel," she choked, and she grabbed the phone. "Hello? Hello?"

A dial tone buzzed loudly in her ear. There was no one on the other end.

Yet she could still hear a phone ringing.

Belinda stared down at the receiver, confused.

And then . . . slowly . . . it dawned on her.

This must be another line, a private line for Mr. Thorne's personal use. Separate from the kitchen phone downstairs.

Trembling all over, she ran back to the kitchen, snatching the receiver up breathlessly, praying he hadn't hung up.

"Noel!" she gasped. "Hello?"

"Is that you, Miss Belinda?" Cobbs sounded surprised.

"Oh, Cobbs, thank God." She was holding the phone so tight, so very tight to keep from dropping it, to keep from falling apart, and her voice came out, a hysterical stranger she didn't know — "Cobbs, I've got to talk to Noel — it's important —"

"But he isn't here, miss — I was just going to ask you where —"

"But that's impossible," Belinda broke in. "He should have been there by now. Adam called and said he should come —"

"Adam, miss?"

"Yes, at the hospital and —"

"Mister Adam's not here. There's no one here but me."

Cobbs's voice faded, and Belinda stared at the phone, holding it away from her like something lethal. She could hear her name being repeated over and over again, and as she stood there, frozen, Sasha rose to her feet, hair prickling as she gave a low, deep snarl.

Belinda dropped the phone.

It swung back and forth on its cord . . . banging . . . banging against the wall.

Somewhere in the house a door opened.

And a foot dragged slowly along a hall.

He's in the house.

He's in the house and he's been here the whole time.

Belinda backed up, her hands reaching behind her for the patio doors, her eyes glued in terror on the opposite doorway and the empty corridor beyond. She felt the handle, and her fingers closed around it. She pulled it and it held . . . she gave it a jerk and it swung wide — with a cry she whirled around —

Adam filled the doorway.

In the half shadows he looked inhuman — his waxy skin and jaggedly stitched face — his eyes black holes. . . .

There was a look of triumph on his face.

With a scream Belinda jumped back, falling into the counter, knocking herself off balance. As she scrambled out of his reach, Sasha barked and ran into the hall, and Belinda went after her, blind with fear. She could hear Adam laughing, deep in his throat, enjoying her panic. As she reached the entryway and sprang for the door, Sasha suddenly bounded forward —

Right into Noel's outstretched arms.

"Hey, Sasha, what's —" The smile died on his lips as Belinda flung herself against him. As he stared uncomprehendingly, Belinda whirled around and saw that the hall behind her was empty.

"Noel — he's *here* —"

"*Ssh* — Belinda, what is it? What's — ?"

"He's *here*, I tell you, we've got to get *out* of here!" She grabbed his arm, dragging him to the door. "*Adam!* He was right behind me — I *swear* it — oh, God, Noel, we've got to get help — he's going to *kill* us — I thought it was just me — but I found the will — he wants to get rid of you, too —"

"Kill —" Noel's face looked pale and stricken. "Belinda — wait — what —"

"I found the will — if your parents die, everything goes to you and to Adam. Oh, Noel, don't you *see*, last night on the road — Adam was trying to kill *you* so he could get all the money! He *did* cause the wreck that night — just like you thought. He killed his own father just like he did his aunt and uncle —"

"My God — Belinda —"

And she was tugging on him, trying to pull him out the door, her eyes fixed wide on the hall, knowing at any second that Adam's face would come out of the shadows —

"Don't you see? I found his handkerchief — it has his initial in the corner — he knows I can identify him with it —"

"The handkerchief," Noel said woodenly.

"*Please!*" Belinda shoved him again but he seemed stunned, gaping at her like he couldn't believe what was happening. "Noel — he's going to *kill* us — we've *got* to go to the police — *now!*"

"His initial," Noel mumbled.

"The A at the top — Adam *was* the one I saw on the hill that night — he was watching the car burn — he's a murderer, don't you *understand* — a —"

And then she saw Noel staring.

And even before she turned around . . . she knew.

Adam's face was watching them from the darkness of the hallway.

And then, to her horror, he moved out into the light.

The cane was gone. He wasn't limping.

"The handkerchief," he said softly. "With the letter A."

Belinda had never been so terrified. She grabbed Noel's arm; it felt stiff and cold. His eyes were pinned on Adam's mutilated face, as if strangely hypnotized.

"The man on the hill," Adam laughed, and it was

a soft, humorless laugh. "The one watching."

"You were supposed to have it done by now," Noel said.

Adam came closer. He was holding an icepick, and he was smiling. "The one whose name starts with A."

"She thinks it's *you*, Adam," Noel said.

"Well, I never did have a face that people trusted. Not like yours . . . Noel *Ashby*."

And as Belinda's heart stopped, as she looked up into Noel's solemn brown eyes, she felt his arm pull away from her touch.

"Put her in the car," Noel said quietly. "It's time for a little reunion."

Chapter 19

"It was you, Noel," Belinda said numbly. "*You* were the one watching that night — the one on the hill. It was *your* handkerchief, not Adam's. But . . . why?"

"It was so perfect," Adam muttered. "Noel's idea . . . and so damn *perfect*. Everything timed . . . right down to the exact second . . . the exact spot on the road. And then we came across *you*. Even after I passed your car, you kept right on my tail . . . and then . . ." A look of bewilderment crossed his face. "Everyone in the car started to panic — I couldn't concentrate — the place I should have jumped out — somehow I passed it — and then —"

"Get in the car," Noel said. "Let's get this thing over with."

"What are you going to do to me?" Belinda asked fearfully.

Adam's hand went to his face. "Noel couldn't even check to see if I was all right. You wouldn't leave. You wouldn't leave, but you wouldn't help."

"I wanted to help," Belinda cried. "I *tried* to help, but they wouldn't let me — and — and the car —"

"Blew," Adam nodded. "I know. I watched it. I watched it, and I tried to hold my face together. . . ." He put the icepick to her cheek and trailed it, ever so softly, over her skin. "Have you ever had your face sliced open? Do you know how it feels?"

"We're wasting time," Noel said. He backed toward the door. He looked pale and strained and impatient.

"Rip . . . rip . . . rip." As he spoke, Adam moved the point gently back and forth over Belinda's face. "And you try to scream, but there's blood, choking you . . . and you try to see . . . you try to breathe . . . and there's just blood. And you wonder if you even look human anymore —"

"I wanted to help," Belinda whispered.

Adam laughed softly. "You wanted to help. Teaching me English and math . . . feeling sorry for me." His eyes flared for an instant, then just as quickly died. "Sloppy job," he whispered. "Sloppy, sloppy job. I almost didn't make it out of there, you know that? You almost killed me. On my *birthday*. April first. That's right, Belinda. April *first*. What a way to celebrate, huh? Over the cliff — and I'm a millionaire! But I almost didn't *live* to be eighteen. And all because of you."

"I didn't mean — you've got to believe —"

"We're going," Noel said. "We're going right now. I mean it."

"I never forget," Adam gave a wry smile. "I never forget, and I never forgive." The smile widened. "But I don't like to rush, either. It's so much more pleasant to just take my time — that way it goes right, the way it's supposed to."

"Please," Belinda began, but he shoved her out the door.

"Go on. Let's take a ride."

She wasn't even aware of getting into the car. She felt hands on her, pushing her, rough hands with grips like steel — and suddenly there were houses going by, houses with lights on in windows, where everyone inside was safe. . . .

"You should have let me do it my way," Adam sighed. "It would have been a lot more fun."

"Shut up." Noel steered the car expertly through the hazy streets, his eyes calm as he scanned the sidewalks, missing nothing. Wedged in between them, Belinda felt the merciless hold of Adam's arm around her shoulders, and she felt like she was going to faint. He was amazingly strong for his slenderness. She thought of the snake in her bed, the snake around Adam's neck that night, their supple bodies pulsing with brick-hard muscle . . . how simple for them, to crush and to kill. . . .

"Where's Hildy?" She'd wanted to ask for so long, had been so afraid of the answer.

On her left side, Noel glanced at Adam, but only with mild curiosity.

Adam smiled. "Don't worry. You'll all be together again before you know it."

Belinda squeezed her eyes shut . . . forced horrible images away. "And Frank? They're alive?"

"Let's just say . . ." Adam thought a moment — "for the time being."

Over her head Adam looked at Noel, but when Noel didn't reply, Adam's eyes slid back to the road. Other than the whisper of tires on wet pavement, there was no sound. Belinda tried to move her cramped arms, and Adam's grip immediately tightened. She bit her lip and forced back a scream.

"I trusted you, Noel," she said softly.

In the pale glow of passing lights, Noel's cheeks tightened, his mouth pressing into a hard line. He stepped on the accelerator and swerved around a curve, throwing Belinda hard into Adam. Adam's eyes went over her in warning.

"People will know," she said at last. "My mother saw us leave together, she —"

One of Adam's hands crept around her neck . . . the other pressed the icepick into her side. She cried out in pain and surprise.

"Stop it," Noel said calmly to Adam. "Don't do anything to her yet."

"Then make her be quiet."

"They'll catch you," Belinda said. "Sooner or later —"

"No one will catch us," Adam corrected her. "No one will catch us because no one will know. And by the time they find you and your friends . . ."

"Where are we going?" Belinda's eyes strained through the night. "Where are you taking me?"

"I wish you hadn't been there," Noel said suddenly. His hands tightened on the wheel and he sounded angry. "I wish you'd never gotten involved."

"I told you this was business," Adam said irritably. "Don't apologize to her."

"She wasn't driving," Noel said, and Adam's glance was sharp. "She wasn't driving the car. The other girl was."

"It doesn't matter," Adam said. "They're *all* responsible for what happened."

"It wasn't your fault," Noel said to Belinda, but not unkindly. "I saw you get out. You tried to help, but you couldn't."

"Stop talking to her," Adam said. He pressed harder on Belinda's windpipe and she gagged. "It's all timing, you know. Like a well-planned stunt." His voice went chillingly calm. "I pick them up from the airport . . . I drive them back home . . . except they never get home because the car misses a curve. . . ." His eyes angled down, full of hate. "But if the stunt's off by a split second, then someone gets hurt. First you get in our way . . . and the old man doesn't die right then — he doesn't die in the fire like he's supposed to. And dear old Gloria. Can you believe it? It should have been different . . . it shouldn't have ended up like this —"

"Frank kept grabbing the wheel," Belinda was pleading now, trying to make him understand. "He was playing a joke — Hildy and I tried to stop him —"

"So perfect. So many times on that road, I knew it by heart. Just where I could jump out and the car could go over." Adam half smiled. "I've done it before, you know. I'm very good at it." His fingers tensed, and she began to cough.

"Stop," Belinda whimpered, "you're hurting me —"

"Let her go, Adam," Noel said.

"But it was easy to find you," Adam seemed calmer now, reasonable. "Yes, it was real easy to find you. That high school sticker on your car . . . and your stupid friends shouting your name — Noel saw all of it — heard all of it — he was following me . . . coming to pick me up." Adam looked amused. "And then you advertised everywhere in town . . . like you *wanted* me to find you, you know? And that stupid librarian even showed Noel your picture. Yes . . . you were easy to find."

"You're the one," Belinda looked up at Noel. "You're the one who was asking questions about me —"

"But we couldn't be sure," Adam went on, rubbing his finger over his upper lip. He ran the icepick slowly down her side, puncturing her blouse . . . piercing her skin. "We couldn't be sure how much you knew . . . that's why we had to watch you . . . get to know you. And you didn't know about my car, so it was easy to follow you."

Noel turned off the road. They were heading out of town now, up into the hills. It was darker here . . . not a car in sight.

"But the handkerchief." Adam shook his head. "You picked up Noel's handkerchief, and now you know what happened —"

"I've never told anyone about that night." Belinda grasped at straws. "And I *won't* tell anyone — not ever —"

Noel's glance silenced her. "You told me."

He stopped the car and opened his door.

"Get out," he said.

This isn't real . . . this isn't happening.

"Please — you've got to believe me — we didn't mean —"

"Move."

Wind lashed at her as she stumbled out onto the road. There was no moon, but Noel waved the thin beam of a flashlight at her feet.

"Look familiar?" Adam said casually, giving her a push from behind.

As the pale light swept out ahead of her, Belinda saw the dirt road angling straight down, swallowed up in a sea of gray fog. She knew where she was now. She knew that somewhere within that swirling mass, the road made a hairpin curve . . . and beyond that, a sudden plunge went down and down forever. . . .

"Suicide Drop," the words choked out and she spun around in terror, caught once more in Adam's merciless grip.

"Clever girl," he whispered. "But doesn't it remind you of something else? Another road on another night not so different from this?"

Belinda had a sudden, strange feeling of being outside herself — of watching herself floating, trapped in Adam's arms. She could feel her shredded blouse, warm and sticky against her side . . . her body numb with someone else's pain. Her throat felt raw and swollen . . . she heard her own breath rasping in her throat . . . yet it seemed like someone else who was crying.

"Over there," Noel said, and Adam's hold tightened on her again as he pulled her off the road and into some trees behind a massive wall of rock. Belinda recognized the car hidden there, and her heart thudded sickeningly into her stomach.

"Frank!"

"Yell all you want," Adam told her. "He can't hear you."

As they neared the car, Noel opened the door and shone the flashlight in. Frank's prone body lay across the front seat, and as Belinda tried to reach for him, Noel heaved him over and nodded to Adam.

"Get the other one."

Bewildered, Belinda realized that Adam had released her, that Noel's hand had replaced Adam's upon her arm. As her eyes widened, he reached calmly into his jacket and brought out a gun.

"I don't want to use this. Please don't make me."

"Belinda!"

She heard her name and spun around with a cry. Hildy was being thrust toward her, and the two girls collapsed in each other's arms.

"Oh, Hildy —"

"I was on my way to Frank's — and Noel stopped me — he said something terrible had happened to you — I got in the car —"

"*Ssh*, Hildy, don't —"

"They got Frank at the pool and took his car — he's still unconscious — then they put me in the trunk —"

Belinda stared at her in horror. One side of her hair had been savagely chopped off, and her blouse was torn. "Are you hurt? Did they hurt you?"

Hildy opened her mouth but Adam jerked her away. "What? And ruin the happy ending?"

As the girls watched helplessly, Noel handed the gun to Adam and climbed into the front seat. "Walk them down there — just like we planned. I'll bring the car."

"My pleasure." Adam motioned to them, gave a mocking bow. "After you, ladies."

It was hard to see clearly in the feeble glow of the flashlight, but as they made their way down the muddy incline, Belinda sensed that they were getting too close to the edge of the drop. Straining through the fog, she could make out the shape of Frank's car as Noel brought it to a stop, facing the cliff. Adam opened one rear door and pointed his pistol.

"Into the back. Over against the other side."

Belinda couldn't stand it anymore. "What are you doing? Noel!"

As Adam forced her into the car, Noel turned around in the front seat and gave her a long, thoughtful look . . . then put a hand to her cheek and gently wiped her tears.

"I wanted to let you go," he explained softly. "I wanted to call it even —"

"She knows everything!" Adam spat at him. "Are you crazy?"

From the corner of her eye, she could see the gun moving . . . Hildy falling in after her . . .

"But you understand why I can't," Noel went on logically. He pulled Frank's body closer, propping his head on the dashboard. "It won't take long. You won't have time to get out before Adam pushes you over the cliff."

"Six inches," Adam said, smiling. "Six inches from the edge. How many seconds in six . . . slippery . . . inches?"

"Don't," Hildy sobbed. "Please don't kill us — don't leave us here —"

"But you won't be alone!" Adam feigned surprise. "We wouldn't be that rude, would we, Noel, to leave them here alone the way they left me? Dear old Gloria will be waiting down there for you — uh — you *do* remember where you dumped her, don't you, Noel?"

"You killed your mother," Belinda's voice was a dull whisper. "That day you took her to the airport — you brought her here instead — and all this time —"

"*Noel?*" Adam sounded annoyed. "Noel's great at making plans, but he doesn't have much of a stomach for carrying them out . . . *I* was the one who —"

"Stop it, Adam," Noel said quietly. "Just quit talking, and do what you have to do."

"Noel, please." Belinda looked into his eyes, the

gentle eyes so calm and so resolved. "Please don't do this —"

Adam slammed the back door.

"Push it over," Noel mumbled. He started to get out, his body crouched on the edge of the seat, ghostlike in the shadows.

Adam grinned in at them through the window.

And pointed the gun at Noel's face.

"Close the door," he said. "You're not going anywhere."

For a split instant everything froze. Belinda saw Noel's look of disbelief . . . the leering triumph of Adam as he clicked back the hammer.

"April Fools'," Adam hissed. "The joke's on you."

"*No!*" Belinda screamed.

Noel's door flew open, knocking Adam off balance. Cursing, Adam fell backward, the gun sailing through the air, as Noel landed on top of him. The fog was so thick now that Belinda couldn't see anything out the windows — but she could hear the thuds and groans of a scuffle . . . and she could hear Hildy's rising hysteria.

"We're *moving*, Belinda! And the doors won't open — they're locked or something!"

"We'll have to get out the front!" Desperately, Belinda angled herself over the seat, trying to move Frank, to reach the handle. The door shivered in the wind and blew open.

"We have to crawl over! Come on — *hurry!*"

"I can't — I —" Hildy shrieked as something hit them from behind. Belinda toppled back down beside her, gazing in horror out the back windshield as Noel slammed Adam up against the trunk.

They felt the car rock forward, mud giving way beneath the wheels.

"*Hildy! Come on!*" In sheer panic, Belinda scrambled into the front, giving Frank a shove toward the door. "Hildy — *please* —"

Frank's body stuck across the doorway. Belinda heard Hildy's sobs, felt Hildy's arms flailing behind her as they both tried to dislodge Frank and roll him through the door.

And then they started to slide.

Belinda's head swiveled — she saw Hildy looking at her with a horrible, helpless understanding —

"Belinda —" she choked.

And "*Belinda!*" someone echoed. "*Belinda! Hang on!*"

In slow motion, Belinda saw Frank's body suddenly disappear, heard the back door burst open. As she stared, dazed, a pair of strong arms suddenly grabbed her and jerked her free. She saw a nightmare kaleidoscope of black night, Hildy sprawled on the ground, and whirlpools of red and blue lights, reflected in the thick, wet fog.

The car went over the drop.

Suddenly there were voices . . . cars . . . people running . . . and Noel holding her.

"Freeze! Police!"

"Okay, son — move away from there — put the girl down — nice and easy —"

"*You* — step *back!* Put your hands where I can see them —"

"Miss Belinda — oh, Miss Belinda, are you quite all right?"

The world slowed . . . righted itself . . . air, cold and real upon her face . . . the swirling rainbows, police lights . . . the ground hard and safe beneath her. She swayed and realized that no one had hold of her now, and then she took one unsteady step as a familiar old face materialized out of the mist.

"Cobbs . . . is that really you?"

"Yes, miss. Sit down now, miss, you're going to be right as rain —"

"But — but how did you know? How did you find me?"

"Ah, Miss Belinda, you underestimate me, I fear." Cobbs's look was reproachful, but there was a touch of pride in his tone. "It was the telephone call. I'd thought all along there was skulduggery going on with those two — but when I called you tonight, things finally began falling into place. I drove immediately to the house — just in time to see them escorting you into a car I didn't recognize. So I followed. And then" — he nodded solemnly — "I rang the police straightaway. On the car telephone."

"Oh, Cobbs." Belinda shook her head, too drained to move. "Where's Hildy?"

"I do believe they're tending to her now."

"Is she all right? And Frank? Are they — ?" Belinda broke off at the sudden sound of upraised voices. Several yards away five policemen were dragging Adam into a patrol car, his bloody face twisted in rage.

Belinda turned away, her eyes desperately searching the darkness.

And then she found him.

Noel was standing quietly, handcuffed between two policemen. As Belinda watched, he suddenly turned and looked at her, his eyes full upon her face. He made no effort to struggle. As his lips moved soundlessly, he took a step toward her, but they jerked him back.

Tears rolled down Belinda's cheeks as the policemen pulled Noel away from her. He looked back over his shoulder, resigned somehow . . . very tired.

"Noel," she whispered.

But he said nothing.

And then he was gone.

Chapter 20

"I've decided you can have Frank," Hildy said.

Belinda glanced up disinterestedly from the couch, her eyes lingering a moment on Hildy's head bowed over a math book. It had been three days now since their ordeal, and she still wasn't used to Hildy's hair cut so short.

"I don't want Frank. I don't want *any* guy. I've decided I really like my life dull and boring."

"Huh. *Frank's* been pretty dull and boring lately. He doesn't remember much, but he's awfully quiet these days." Hildy lowered her head as Belinda went back to her notes. "Belinda . . . I haven't been a good friend."

"Oh, Hildy, stop it —"

"No, really, I haven't, and I know it. When you were scared and upset and needed me to come through for you, I didn't. I was just too scared of losing Frank." She took a deep breath, and her voice sounded sad. "I'm not like you, Belinda. I've always needed someone else to make me feel good about myself."

Belinda smiled at Hildy's woeful expression. "And I'm so together, right?" She chuckled. "Come on, it doesn't matter."

"Yes, it does. I could have lost *you*." Suddenly she reached out and hugged Belinda tight. "I'll be better, okay?"

They pulled apart, smiling, and Belinda gave her a teasing look.

"So where does this leave poor Frank?"

"Well . . . I don't know. At least this new Frank doesn't seem to know any jokes." As Hildy grinned back, her face suddenly softened and she put one hand on Belinda's arm. "And I'm sorry about Noel, Belinda. Honest. I know you really liked him." Cautiously she added, "What's gonna happen to him?"

"Cobbs said Noel and Adam are both going through tests right now — to see if they're competent to stand trial."

"And if they are?"

"Well . . . with Mr. Thorne dead now, and Mrs. Thorne's body recovered . . ." Belinda looked away. "They'll be tried as adults 'cause they're eighteen."

"Well, a lot of good it did them getting all that money when they can't even —" Hildy broke off as the doorbell rang and Belinda went to answer it.

"Cobbs!"

"Good afternoon, miss. I trust you're feeling much improved?"

"Why, yes — come in. I'm so glad to see you —"

"I'm not surprised. I was wondering perhaps if I might speak with Mrs. Swanson?"

"Mom? Sure. Sit down. Would you like some coffee?"

"Not terribly."

"I'd make tea, but I'm afraid it wouldn't come out like yours."

"Undoubtedly not. Then perhaps I should?"

They stared, surpised, as Cobbs went into the kitchen, surveyed it regally, then advanced cautiously toward the dirty stove.

"Good heavens, is it safe to touch?"

"Mr. Cobbs!" said Mrs. Swanson in the doorway behind them. "What a pleasant surprise!"

"Yes, madame," Cobbs acknowledged. "If I might have a moment of your time —"

"Of course. Won't you sit down?"

"I think not. I've come for a reason, so I'll make my point. My professional opinion is that you're sadly in need of domestic service, am I correct?"

Mom's mouth dropped open. Hildy and Belinda looked at each other in delight.

"Service, Mr. Cobbs? Well, really —"

"No offense intended, madame" — his eyes raised in secret appall at the messy kitchen — "but it so happens that I am presently in a position to offer my services."

Mrs. Swanson's expression was somewhere between shocked and amused. "Well, that's very nice of you to think of us, and Belinda's very fond of you —"

"Naturally."

"Please, Mom?" Belinda begged, while Hildy joined in.

"*But*," Mrs. Swanson silenced them both with a look. "I'm afraid we couldn't possibly pay you a decent salary —"

"*Tut, tut*, madame — you bother yourself with trifles. Mr. Frederick Thorne has provided for me most generously in his will, and salary is of little importance to me. What my former employer has also done, by his untimely passing, is to provide me with an abundance of leisure time and no way of filling it."

Mrs. Swanson looked suspicious. She glanced at Belinda and Hildy, who were nodding vigorously.

"Well . . . I . . ."

"It appears to me that Miss Belinda needs a stronger hand," Cobbs went on blandly. "Perhaps then she would find herself in far less trouble" — the eyebrow raised, the eyes settling sternly on Belinda — "*and* make a wiser choice about her men."

This time Mrs. Swanson burst out laughing, and as Cobbs went to the sink and began filling the kettle, she shook her head. "Well . . . since you put it that way — I suppose something could be worked out."

"Splendid."

"And Sasha," Belinda said quickly, "Sasha will have to come, too —"

Cobbs's back went more rigid than usual, and a long-suffering sigh escaped him.

"What man could possibly have a more fulfilled life than I."

As Mrs. Swanson laughed, she put an arm around Hildy and led her into the living room. "Now don't you have a *math* final you're trying very hard to flunk —"

Belinda perched on the counter, her smile fading as Cobbs adjusted the stove. Her mind had been drifting away from her a lot these past few days — thoughts battling each other for space in her head, trying to sort themselves out. When she looked up again, Cobbs was in front of her, with his hand extended.

In it was a handkerchief, the initial A stitched neatly into the corner.

Belinda's eyes filled, and she looked up into wiser ones. "What's — ?"

"Mister Noel said he couldn't think of anything else to give you. He wanted you to have this."

"But —"

"With no bad memories attached, was the way he put it. He said you'd understand."

Belinda took it from him . . . held it against her cheek. "You know . . . for a while I thought *you* were following me?"

"How perceptive of you. It just so happens that I *was*, on several occasions."

"But when I asked you, you said —"

"I didn't see any cause for alarming you." Cobbs looked slightly annoyed.

"You mean, you were watching out for me?"

"*Hmph*. There's absolutely no need for sentimentality, you know. I was merely doing my duty, nothing more, nothing less."

Belinda half smiled at that. "Thanks, then. For doing your duty, I mean." She unfolded the neat square of cloth . . . smoothed it out . . . folded it back again. "You know, Cobbs . . . even after all that's happened . . . I just keep wishing . . ."

"It was the debts," Cobbs said firmly. "It's never enough, you know, once some people get a bit of money. It simply goes to their heads. They need more and more of it. I suppose . . . desperation led from one thing to another."

Belinda nodded . . . pressed the handkerchief to her eyes . . . tried to speak over sudden, choking tears.

"I don't think he ever really meant to kill me . . . I keep thinking . . . deep down inside . . . he didn't really want to —"

She threw her arms around Cobbs . . . buried her face in his coat . . . heard his hoarse whisper as she began to cry.

"Poor child . . . yes . . . cry it all out."

"Oh, Cobbs, he was so special — he tried to save me at the end —"

"Yes, I know."

"And it hurts so bad —"

"The pain, in time, will heal."

"Do you really think so?" she sniffled.

"I'd swear it."

Belinda looked up, and through her tears laughed a little.

"You know something?"

"I know everything."

"I really love you, Cobbs."

And then she felt his hand gently upon her hair.

"And I *you*, miss."

About the Author

RICHIE TANKERSLEY CUSICK is also the best-selling author of the Point paperbacks *Trick or Treat* and *The Lifeguard*.

Ms. Cusick was born on April Fools' Day (no joke!) in New Orleans, Louisiana. She now makes her home just outside Kansas City, Missouri, with her husband, Rick, and their cocker spaniel, Hannah.

MYSTERY THRILLER

Introducing, a new series of hard hitting, action packed thrillers for young adults.

THE SONG OF THE DEAD by Anthony Masters
For the first time in years 'the song of the dead' is heard around the mud flats of Whitstable. But this time is it really the ghostly cries of dead sailors? Or is it something far more sinister? Barney Hampton is sure that something strange is going on – and he's determined to get to the bottom of the mystery . . .

THE FERRYMAN'S SON by Ian Strachan
Rob is convinced that Drewe and Miles are up to no good. Why else would two sleek city whizz-kids want to spend the summer yachting around a sleepy Devonshire village? Where do they go on their frequent night cruises? And why does the lovely Kimberley go with them? Then Kimberley disappears, and Rob finds himself embroiled in a web of deadly intrigue . . .

Further titles to look out for in the Mystery Thriller series:

Treasure of Grey Manor by Terry Deary
The Foggiest by Dave Belbin
Blue Murder by Jay Kelso
Dead Man's Secret by Linda Allen